Friedrich Spielhagen, Levi Sternberg

The German Pioneers

Vol. 1

Friedrich Spielhagen, Levi Sternberg

The German Pioneers
Vol. 1

ISBN/EAN: 9783337343286

Printed in Europe, USA, Canada, Australia, Japan

Cover: Foto ©Andreas Hilbeck / pixelio.de

More available books at **www.hansebooks.com**

THE GERMAN PIONEERS

A TALE OF THE MOHAWK

BY

FREDERICK SPIELHAGEN.

TRANSLATED FROM THE GERMAN BY

THE REV. LEVI STERNBERG, D. D.

CHICAGO:

DONOHUE, HENNEBERRY & CO.

1891.

THE GERMAN PIONEERS

CHAPTER I

On a certain forenoon in the month of April, 1758, there was unusual activity in the harbor of New York. In spite of the disagreeable weather—which had now already lasted two days, with dense fogs and drizzling rain, and even then, from low, gray clouds, was drenching the multitude—there stood upon the quay dense groups of people looking at a large Dutch three-master, which had already lain a couple of days in the roadstead, and now was swinging at anchor in the troubled water nearer shore.

"The gentlemen would have done better to have remained at home," said a little man, referring to two broad-shouldered farmers, who stood near. "I will eat my tailor's goose and not be called Samuel Squenz if, out of the skin-covered skeletons which have thus far passed here on their way to the state-house to take the oath of allegiance to our king—whom may God bless—they can select a single ordinary farm-hand."

"Have you seen them?" asked another, who had just joined the group.

"Have I seen them!" replied Samuel Squenz.

"We have all seen them. I tell you, neighbor, had they come out of the grave after lying there four months they could not have more bones and less flesh. Surely four months in the grave and four months on that Hollander amounts to about the same thing."

"The poor devils!" said the other.

"Ah, what poor devils?" called out a man, distinguished from those around him by his larger wig, more careful dress, rotund body, red, flabby cheeks, and German accent. "Poor devils! What brings them here? What are we to do with the starved ragamuffins, of whom one half could not pay full fare? Now according to our wise laws a wage-sale must be openly made, as was yesterday advertised both in the 'Gazette' and in the 'Journal.'"

"They bring us nothing into the country except the dirty rags they have on and ship-fever, from which may God protect us," called out Samuel Squenz. "I kept nose and mouth shut as the vermin crept past us."

"It is a sin," said neighbor Flint.

"It is a shame," snarled neighbor Bill.

"Therefore I have always said," continued the man, with the red, hanging cheeks, "that we should do as they do in Philadelphia, where for the last thirty years they have levied a poll-tax of forty shillings on every imported Dutchman, just as they do on a nigger. But here a man may preach and preach, but it is to deaf ears. I will not stay out in the rain

on account of these ragamuffins. Good day, gentlemen."

The big man touched his three-cornered hat, but,
instead of leaving the place, went with heavy strides
to the edge of the quay and looked at the ship, which
had by this time raised its anchor and was being
slowly driven on by the tide.

"It is a sin," said neighbor Flint.

"It is a shame," snarled neighbor Bill.

"That is—for Mr. Pitcher to speak so," cried one
who now came up and had heard the last words of
him who was just leaving.

"What do you mean by that, Mr. Brown?" asked
Samuel Squenz, respectfully lifting his cap.

"Isn't it a shame, now," said Mr. Brown, a small,
old, lean man, who spoke with much animation, and
while speaking gesticulated violently with his lean
little arms. "Isn't it a shame for one to speak so
contemptuously about his own countrymen? Is not
this Mr. Pitcher just as good, or as bad as the poor
devils there on the ship? Did not his parents, in
1710, while Robert Hunter was governor, come to
New York with the great immigration, from the Palatinate? They were good, respectable people, whom
I knew well, who had a hard time of it, and who
honestly and honorably worked up to their subse-
quent better condition. They do not deserve that
this, their son, whom I have seen running about the
streets barefoot, should so utterly forget them and

slander their memory as to change his name from the German, Krug, into the English, Pitcher. Pitcher indeed! The old Krug was, I think, made out of better clay than this young English Pitcher, who reviles these immigrants and thereby creeps under the same cover with the Dutch who sell people for a term of years, and deal in human flesh as you do, neighbor Flint, with beef, and you, neighbor Bill, with cheese and butter."

The old man thrust his bamboo cane angrily into the moist ground.

"It is a sin," said neighbor Flint.

"It is a shame," said neighbor Bill.

"With your permission, neighbors," said Samuel Squenz, "I will not praise Mr. Pitcher, though he gives me work. One must, however, honor his father, though he was a miserable Dutchman. Nor will I have anything to do with those who deal in human flesh, or sell people for a term of years. May the Lord forgive Mr. Pitcher if he meddles with such a business. But I cannot blame those to whom this immigration is an open grief, and who declare it to be injurious to the commonwealth. These vagabonds take the bread from our mouths, and stuff it into their unwashed mouths, while they are too stupid or too lazy to earn a shilling."

"Do you see that man near the edge of the quay close to Mr. Pitcher?" said Mr. Brown.

"The young farmer?"

"The same. How do you like him?"

"He is a noble looking fellow, though I cannot approve of the cut of his coat."

"Now this young man is also German, called Lambert Sternberg. He lives on Canada Creek, and I have just, in my office, counted out one hundred pounds into his hands, and have given him a commission for another hundred pounds if he delivers to my correspondents in Albany this fall by October, on my account, the tar and rosin agreed upon."

"Is it possible," said Samuel Squenz. "Yes, yes, there are exceptions."

"Not at all an exception," earnestly replied Mr. Brown. "Lambert Sternberg's brother is a fur-hunter and has, for six years, been in a mutually advantageous partnership with my neighbor Squirrel. So likewise there live on Canada Creek, on the Mohawk, and on the Schoharie dozens, yes, hundreds of excellent people, who have in their veins as pure German blood as you and I have English blood. By diligent labor they have placed themselves in comfortable circumstances; and it would have gone still better with them had not the Government, instead of aiding and protecting them, thrown obstacles in their way. This time the young man was obliged to take his long journey to New York to maintain his and his neighbors' rights to the pine trees growing on their own ground —a right as clear as the sun—and yet, God only knows what the issue would have been, had I not in-

tervened and showed the Governor that the purchaser
of land, first from the Indians, then from the government, should not be forced to buy it again for the third
time from the first swindler who crowds himself in
and manages to get some show of title."

Mr. Brown spoke with great earnestness. Most of
his hearers, whose eyes wandered back and forth between the speaker and the farmer at the edge of the
quay, seemed to be convinced. However Samuel
Squenz would not keep quiet, but cried out with a
grieved voice:

"What do you thus show, Mr. Brown, except that
these scamps swallow up the land to which we, and
our children, and our children's children, are entitled?
And one must not speak of injury done to the commonwealth! I would like to know what else it should
be called?"

"A strengthening," cried Mr. Brown; "a strengthening and an establishing of the commonwealth.
That would be the right word. Is it not a blessing
for us all that outside, on the farthest border, these
poor Germans have settled, and, if God permit, will
settle still farther, and, by their position, are in constant conflict with the French, and whom we have to
thank that you, and I, and all of us here in New
York, can peacefully prosecute our business. When
last fall Captain Belletre, with his French and Indians, fell upon the valley of the Mohawk, who hindered that he did not reach Albany, and God knows

how much further? We did not, for two years ago we allowed Fort Oswego to be taken; and General Abercrombie, who commands at Albany, had done nothing to protect the threatened points until October when Belletre came. I ask again, who hindered? The Germans, who fought as well as they could under the lead of their watchful captain, Nicolas Herkimer, though they lost forty killed and one hundred and two prisoners, not to speak of the $50,000 damage done by the thieving, burning murderers. That is an injury to the commonwealth, Mr. Squenz, of which you may take occasion to think, Mr. Squenz, and therewith I commend you to God."

The choleric old gentleman had spoken in such a passion that, in spite of the rain, he took off, not only his hat, but also his wig, and was now wiping his bald head with his handkerchief as he left the group and shuffled over to the young countryman, who still stood in the same place on the quay looking at the ship. Now, however, as the old man patted him on the shoulder, he turned about with the appearance of one who has just been awakened out of a dream. It could not have been a pleasant dream. On the fine, dark-complexioned face there was a trace of deep grief, and the large, blue, kind, German eyes looked very sad.

"Ah, Mr. Brown," said the young man, "I supposed you had long since gone home."

"While I stood but ten steps behind you and spent

my breath in defending you! But so it is with you Germans. To strike home when it comes to the worst—that you can do; but to speak for yourselves —to maintain your rights against the simpletons who look at you over the shoulder and who shrug the shoulder over you—that you leave for others."

"What has happened, Mr. Brown?" said the young man.

"What has happened! The old story. I have again rushed into the fire for you sleepy fellows— I, an old fool. Do you think—but for this morning I have already vexed myself enough on your account, and I can surely reckon on having an attack of the colic this evening. And this weather besides— the devil take the weather, and the Germans too! Come, Mr. Lambert, come."

The old man moved about uneasily.

"I would like to stay a little longer," said Lambert, hanging back.

"You have no time to lose if you mean to go by the Albany boat. It leaves at three o'clock, and you also wanted to get your horse shod."

Lambert turned from the ship, which by this time had come quite near, to his business friend, and from him again to the ship.

"If you will permit me," said Lambert.

"Do as you please," cried the old man. "You may look at your countrymen and spoil your appetite for dinner. Or you may buy a young blockhead who will

eat the hair off your head, or a handsome maid who
would not behave at home, but is naturally good
enough for you—or perhaps rather two—that your
brother Conrad may also be provided for.   Do as you
please, but let me go home.   We eat at twelve, and
Mrs. Brown likes her guests to be punctual.   Good
morning."

Mr. Brown held down his hat, which the wind
threatened to take off, with his bamboo cane, and
hurried away at the moment when a dull sound from
Broadway indicated that the immigrants were returning.

CHAPTER II

There entered new life into the wet and surly groups on the quay. Men stood on tiptoe and eagerly looked in the direction of Broadway, where the wretched crowd now appeared. Others pressed forward to the point where the ship was to land. It was now so near that they were already casting over the ropes. Lambert, who still stood on the outer edge, saw himself surrounded by a dense mass, and thus kept in a place he would now have gladly surrendered to anyone whose eyes and heart could better endure the sight of the utmost human wretchedness.

The scene of this misery was the deck of the ship above and below, of which he now had an unobstructed view. Already, from a distance, had the confusion caused by the commingled piles of bales, casks, trunks, and baskets, between which wives and children were wandering about, filled him with sad reflections. But his heart ceased to beat and his chest to heave as, clearer and clearer, and now also very near, the crying and scolding, weeping and lamenting of the unfortunate people struck upon his ear. As his glance wandered from one pitiable object to another, he everywhere saw countenances deathly pale and disfigured by hunger and sickness, out of

14

whose deep, sunken eyes dull despair and frenzied
anxiety fearfully glared. As they thus stood in motionless groups it seemed as if they had lost all power
and inclination to do anything for themselves. Their
heads were stretched forward like timid sheep which
the butcher's dog has driven to the door of the slaugh-
ter house. Thus they hastened and hurried and
crowded between the chests and casks, and greedily
gathered up their poor belongings. Elsewhere, in
confused quarreling and strife, they snatched bundles
from each other, and threatened each other with their
fists, until the supercargo intervened and with scolding and pushing and striking, separated them. Lambert could endure the horrible sight no longer, and
pressed back the crowd which now surrounded him
like a wall. As he involuntarily cast a last glance
over the deck it fell upon a form which he had not
before noticed, and at once he stopped as though
struck by lightning.

Directly before him there leaned against a great
pile of bales a young, tall, slender maiden. Her right
arm was thrust against the bales, the hand supporting her head. Her other arm hung at her side. Her
face, of which he had only a side view, was so thin
and pale that the long, dark eyelashes were brought
out with singular distinctness. The lustrous black
hair was wound around the head in comely braids,
and her dress, though poor and threadbare enough,
was more tasty than that of the other women, to

whom she was evidently greatly superior in refinement. As though a powerful enchantment had seized him, Lambert could not withdraw his gaze from this face. He had never seen anything so beautiful. He had not thought that anything so beautiful could be found. Nearly breathless, without knowing what he was doing—even forgetting where he was—he looked at the stranger as though she were an apparition, until, with sad shaking of the head, she let her supporting arm fall and, passing around the pile of goods against which she had leaned, she disappeared from his sight.

At this moment, back on the Battery, there sounded a great shouting and drumming and fifing. The crowd pressed forward, and was again pushed back. The police who accompanied the immigrants had already had trouble with the mob all the way through the city, and now, having to pass through the compact mass on the quay to the gang-plank, were obliged to use all their authority and to swing their clubs indiscriminately. So it happened that over the living wall before him Lambert saw now and then a pale, grief-stricken countenance, as the poor immigrants passed over the narrow gangway to the deck of the ship. Here those who had just returned on board immediately began to call for their wives and children, some of whom, overcome by fatigue, did not move, while others hastened to their husbands as soon as possible. A dreadful confusion arose,

which was increased by the ship's crew rushing into
the crowd and making room by pushing and striking
indiscriminately. It had reached its highest point
when those on the quay, headed by the stout Mr.
Pitcher, in a close mass pushed on from behind and
blocked up the way to every one who, with his bundles and packs, desired to leave the ship. The men
screamed, the women cried, the children whimpered,
the captain and sailors cursed and swore. The police
swung their clubs. It was a dreadful chaos, in which
Lambert's anxious glances were ever peering about for
the poor girl who was looking on the tumult which
was roaring around her, so lonely, so forsaken, so
still and patient. As he saw her form again emerge,
now on the forward part of the deck, he held back no
longer. Without further thought, with a mighty
spring from the edge of the quay, he swung himself
aboard of the ship and hastened to the point where
he had last seen her. He knew not why he did this.
He had no conception of what he should say to the
maiden when he should reach her. It seemed as
though he was drawn by unseen hands, which it was
impossible for him to resist, and to whose guidance
he willingly committed himself.

After he had approached her, lost sight of her,
feared at last that he should not again find her, he
suddenly came near her. She had kneeled on the
deck before a couple of children—a boy and a girl
from six to eight years old—whose threadbare gar-

ments she was fixing, and was speaking to a woman who stood near with quite a small child in her arms, and who was constantly scolding, till the husband came up and dragged the children away, scolding and cursing. His wife followed him without a word or look of thanks to her who was left behind. She slowly arose and looked sadly at those who were leaving. She followed them, tied a small piece of cloth which she had worn, about the neck of the smallest child, and then slowly returned to the place where the family had left her. Her countenance was more sad than before. Tears rolled over her pale cheeks.

"Can I be of any help to you, madam?" asked Lambert.

The girl raised her dark eyelashes, and looked searchingly with her large brown eyes at his kind, honorable face.

"Nobody can help me," said she.

"Have you no parents, no relatives, no friends?" asked Lambert.

"I have nobody—nobody," replied the maiden, and turned herself partly away that she might hide the tears which now burst forth in streams from her eyes.

Lambert's eyes also became moist. The trouble of the poor girl pressed heavily on his heart.

"Can you not leave the ship?" he further inquired.

The unhappy one, without answering, only wept the more.

"Do not consider me too pressing, kind maiden,

I have seen you standing so forsaken that my pity
has been awakened. And now you yourself say
that you are alone, that you have nobody to help
you, and that nobody can help you. Perhaps I can
do so if you will confide in me. I will surely do all
that is in my power."

While the young man thus spoke the girl wept
more and more gently. She now again turned her
pale face to him and said:

"I thank you, kind man. I thank you with my
whole heart, and may God bless you for the compassion you have felt for a poor, helpless creature. But
help—that indeed you cannot. Who could help me?
By whose help could I leave this ship?"

Her countenance took on an unusual expression.
She looked, with staring eyes, over the bulwarks
into the water which rose and fell at the ship's bow.
"For me there is but one means of escape," she
murmured.

At this moment a man, cursing, pressed through the
crowd, which made room for him in all directions. He
was an under-sized, broad-shouldered fellow with a
red wig, a brutal countenance and a pair of green
eyes which glittered maliciously.

He put on quite an air, dressed in his ship uniform,
and drew after him a sturdy farmer, who seemed to
follow him reluctantly and who looked at the maiden
with dull, staring eyes, while he in the uniform approached, and with legs spread apart, called out in
poor German:

"So, Miss Catherine Weise, I have soon picked up a man.   He is the richest farmer within ten miles, as he says himself, and needs a capable maid-servant on his farm.   He has already bid forty on my bare recommendation.   That indeed is scarcely the half, but perhaps he will now give the whole amount, after he has himself seen you, and has convinced himself that I did not lie to him.   What do you think, Mr. Triller? Isn't she a stunner?   Are you now willing to fork over, ha?"

He struck the farmer on the shoulder and broke out in uproarious laughter.

"Let it be forty-five, captain," said the farmer, "and I'll take her as she stands."

"Not a shilling under ninety," cried the captain, "not a shilling, even if I should have to keep her myself.   No, she would gladly stay with me.   Isn't it true, Miss Catherine?   She is a stunner."

"Don't touch her; if you don't want your skull cracked!" cried Lambert.

The captain took a step back and stared at the young farmer, whom he had not before noticed, and who now stood before him with glowing eyes and balled fists.

"Oho!" he exclaimed, "who are you?   Do you know that I am Captain Van Broom?   Do you know that I shall at once throw you into the water?   What is your name?   What do you want?"

He took a step back, having said the last words in

a far less confident tone. He did not think it prudent to have anything further to do with a man of so
resolute an appearance and so evidently superior to
himself in bodily strength.

"My name is Lambert Sternberg, from Canada
Creek," said the young man. "There live in the
city of New York respectable citizens who know me
well; and what I want I will soon tell you, if you
will kindly step aside with me for a few moments."

"As you wish; as you wish," snarled the captain.

"In a moment," said Lambert. He approached
the maiden, who stood trembling violently, and said
to her in a low tone, "Catherine Weise, will you accept me as your protector, and permit me to do for
you what, under such circumstances, an honorable
man should do for a helpless maiden?"

A deep blush spread over Catherine's face She
fixed her dark eyes upon her questioner with a peculiar expression that made his inmost heart flutter.
She tried to answer, but there came no sound from
her trembling lips.

"Wait here for me," said the young man.

He turned to the captain and went with him to a
retired part of the deck. The robust farmer had
turned aside and felt no further interest in the deal,
after he saw that another purchaser for the merchan-
dise was found, and which, all things considered, was
entirely too dear for him.

"Now, Mr. Broom," said Lambert, as he overtook
him, "I am at your service."

"I'll be —— if I know what you want," said the captain.

"Simply this: To take that girl there, whom you call Catherine Weise, with me from the ship, and that at once."

"Oho!" said the captain, "you are in a hurry. Has she told you how much she owes us?"

"No," said Lambert, "but I have already heard the amount from you."

"Ninety pounds! sir, ninety pounds! That isn't a small matter," cried the captain.

"I suppose you will be able to show that the maiden owes you so much. You will then find me ready."

The captain cast a grim side-glance at the young man like a hyena driven from his prey by a leopard. He would have liked to have the beautiful booty for himself, but was far too shrewd a business man not to avail himself of such a chance. Besides, the Messrs. Van Sluiten and Co., in Rotterdam, and Mr. Pitcher, who was probably now in the ship's office engaged with the book-keeper, had also a word to say. So he spoke in what was for him an unusually courteous tone, instead of the coarse one he had just used:

"If I can show it?—yes, sir. For what do you take Captain Van Broom? With us about everything is booked twice, sir, in farthings and pence. Are you surprised that the amount is so large? I will make it clear. The girl is the daughter of the Rev. Mr. Weise, who died eight days ago, and was buried with

all honor at sea. He was a preacher in the region from
which most of my passengers come. On the way, I
must say it of him, he put himself to a good deal of
trouble for his filthy people and did for them more
than his strength would bear, while they in South-
ampton suffered with hunger and cold; and now on
the voyage provisions with us became somewhat
scarce, and the water—well, one has a heart in his
breast, and I yielded to the preacher when he came
to borrow for his people. So it has happened that
his account has run up a little higher than is usual.
At the best not much was to be got from the old
man, though there still remained the girl, for whom
doubtless a purchaser could be found. So I have
taken the risk, and have by degrees given them credit
for a hundred pounds."

"You before said ninety."

"A hundred pounds, by ——!" shrieked the captain.
"Come with me into the office. There I will show
you in black and white. You, there, supercargo, see
to it that the thieving vagabonds do not slip from
aboard. And you, Mr. Jones, do not leave the gang-
plank; and keep with you Jean and Jacob, and knock
any one down who tries to leave the ship without a
pass. Should any one ask for me, he must wait a
moment. I have to speak with this gentleman. Will
you follow me, Mr. Sternberg?"

The captain opened the door of a low and spacious
cabin which was built on the deck. A dark-complex-

ioned man, with immense brass rings in his ears, sat at a table covered with thick books and papers, diligently writing. Near him stood Mr. Pitcher, with his red, bloated, flabby cheeks, and on his wig-covered head his three-cornered hat, looking over his ·shoulder.

"Ah!" said the captain, "here you are, too, Mr. Pitcher. That fits charmingly. Now we can make the matter clear at once. This is Mr. Charles Pitcher, our general agent for New York. This—"

"I think I already have the honor," said Mr. Pitcher, lifting his hat. "Are not you Mr. Sternberg from Canada Creek, whom I met two years ago in Albany? Have you transacted your business with Mr. Brown? I lately saw you with him on Broadway. Well, other people want to live too. Excuse me, Mr. Sternberg; excuse me. Take a seat. What brings you to us at this time, Mr. Sternberg?"

"It is on account of Catherine Weise," said the captain, in whose eyes the simple countryman, with whom the rich Mr. Pitcher desired to have dealings, had assumed a quite different appearance. "I told you about her yesterday, Mr. Pitcher."

Between Mr. Pitcher and the captain there now took place a short but earnest conversation, of which Lambert understood nothing, as it was carried on in Dutch. They ought to have let the girl go free, but the hateful man at the desk opened a large book and said: "Catherine Weise, folio 470 to 475, beginning

September sixth of last year, in Rotterdam, brought until to day, April fifteenth, 1758, port of New York, amounting to £89, 10s.—"

"Ninety-nine pounds," corrected Captain Van Broom.

"Ninety-nine pounds," repeated the man with the ear-rings. "The gentleman will require a conveyance from us to which the proper signatures are attached. For this we charge one pound. Here is the form. Please give me the specifications as I write."

The dark-complexioned man took a sheet of parchment and read, in a leaden, business-like voice:

"*In nomine dei:* Between Lambert Sternberg, of Canada Creek, and Joanna Catherine Weise, of Zellerfeld, in the electorate of Hanover, aged twenty years, single, the following service contract—shall we say six years, Mr. Sternberg? It is the usual period —for six successive years from this date, under the following conditions mutually agreed upon:

"*Pro primo:* Joanna Catherine Weise, born, etc.; agrees of her own free will, and after due consideration, to bind herself to Mr. Lambert Sternberg to go with him, or under his direction, to West Canada Creek, in the province of New York, and there, from the day on which she shall have arrived in the before-named district, for six successive years to give him true and faithful required maid-service, under no pretense to relax it, much less, without the consent of Lambert Sternberg, to forsake his service.

"To this, *pro secundo*, Lambert Sternberg promises—"

"It is enough," said Lambert.

"How?" said he with the ear-rings.

"It is enough," said Lambert. "I wish first to talk
over the conditions with the maiden."

"My dear sir, consider the circumstances," called
out Mr. Pitcher, in a friendly, helpful tone. "When
a man pays £99 he can dictate the conditions."

"That may be," replied Lambert. "However, it is
my privilege to deal in my own way."

"As you wish—altogether as you wish," said Mr.
Pitcher. "We force nobody. You also wish—"

"Simply a receipt in full for Catherine Weise."

"As you please," said Mr. Pitcher.

While he with the ear-rings wrote out the receipt,
and Lambert counted out the money on the table—
it was the same that he had received an hour before
from Mr. Brown—Mr. Pitcher and the captain grim-
aced sneeringly behind the back of the simpleton who
was so easily limed, and never once looked at the
famous account he was satisfying.

"So," said Mr. Pitcher, "this is finished. Now we
will—"

"Drink to your happy journey," said the captain,
as he reached for a rum-flask which stood near on
the rack.

"And to the *et cetera, et cetera*," cried Mr. Pitcher.

"Good morning, Messrs.," said Lambert, gathering

up the receipt, the half-finished contract and Cathe-rine's passage-ticket, and hurrying out of the cabin as though the deck under him was afire. Brutal laugh-ter rung behind him. He stood still a moment. His cheeks glowed. His heart beat furiously against his ribs. Every convulsed fiber of his body urged him to turn back and take vengeance on the mean scoun-drels for their laughter. But he thought of the poor girl—how much more she had endured, and that he could do nothing better for her than to release her from such a hell, as soon as possible.

The deck had now been somewhat cleared. The more fortunate ones, who needed not to fear the book in the hands of the man with the ear-rings, had already left the ship. Those who were obliged to stay sat and stood around in groups. Stupid indiffer-ence or uncertainty characterized their wan appear-ance. Curious gazers moved about among them, some of whom had come desirous of making contracts similar to the one which lay crushed in Lambert's coat-pocket. The heavy farmer, who had before made a bid on Catherine, was now speaking with another girl, who had adorned her rags with a couple of red ties, and laughed heartily at the broken Ger-man, and at the jokes of the man. They seemed to be already agreed on a bargain.

Lambert hastened as fast as he could to the far-ther part of the deck, where he had already seen Catherine in the same place where he had left her.

But as he came near her he stopped. It seemed to him that nothing had yet been accomplished—that all yet remained to be done. She now turned and saw him. A melancholy smile spread over her countenance.

"Is it not true? Nobody can help me," said she.

"Here is your receipt and your ticket," said Lambert.

His strong, brown hands shook as he gave her the papers, and her thin white hands trembled as she took them. A burning red spread over her countenance.

"Have you done this for me?" said she.

Lambert did not reply, and was greatly agitated as she immediately bowed down, caught his hands and pressed them against her weeping face and lips.

"Kind maiden—kind maiden! what are you doing?" stammered Lambert. "Don't weep. I was glad to do it. I am fortunate to have been able to render you this service. Were it possible I would do the same for all the other unfortunates here. But now let us away. I have but a few hours left. I must begin my homeward journey. I would be glad first to know that you are in safety. Do you know anyone in the city, or in its vicinity to whom I can take you?"

Catherine shook her head.

"Have you no friends among the immigrants who perhaps expect you to accompany them on their farther journey?"

"I have nobody—nobody!" said the girl. "You see everyone thinks only of himself, and alas! everybody has enough of his own to look after."

Lambert stood helpless. He thought for a moment about his old business friend, Mr. Brown. But, alas! Mrs. Brown was not a kind woman. To her, her husband's predilection for the Germans seemed very ridiculous. It did not very well please her to welcome strangers. He knew no other house in the city, except the inn where he had left his horse, and which in other respects was not desirable, especially as to the company which gathered there. He looked at Catherine as though advice must come from her, but her eyes had an anxious and strained expression.

"Do you mean to give me over to other people?" said she.

"What do you mean?" asked Lambert.

"Kind sir, you have already done so much for me, and are reluctant now to tell me that you can do no more for me. I will need a long, long time with my service to pay the heavy debt. I know it well. But I would cheerfully serve you and your parents as long as I live, and even give my life for you. Now you wish to take me to others. Speak freely. I will gladly bind myself for as many years as they desire and make good your recommendation." She smiled sadly and picked up a small bundle that lay near her. "I am ready," said she.

"Catherine!" said Lambert.

She looked inquiringly at him.

"Catherine!" said he again. His chest heaved and fell as though he was summoning up all his strength to speak calmly. "I live far from here, full twenty days' travel, on the utmost border, the farthest settler, in an impoverished region, open to the inroad of our enemies, and which last year suffered from them a dreadful visitation. But if you will go with me—"

A joyful perplexity showed itself in Catherine's wan face.

"How can you ask?" said she.

"Well may I ask," replied Lambert, "and well must I ask. It remains with you. Your evidence of indebtedness is in your own hands and I will never again take it in mine. You are free to come and to go. And so, Catherine Weise, I ask you once more, will you as a free maiden go with me to my home, if I promise you on the honor of a man that I will care for you, help and protect you as a brother should his sister?"

"I will go with you, Lambert Sternberg," said Catherine.

Breathing deeply, she laid her hand in his offered right hand.

Then they hastened over the deck. Catherine nodded tearfully to one and another. She could not speak. Her heart was too full for speech. No one returned her silent farewell, except with dumb and hopeless looks which cut her to the heart. On the long and terrible journey from her home until now, according to her strength and beyond her strength, she had tried to mitigate the boundless wretchedness around her. She could do no more than leave the hapless creatures to their fate. Alas! what a fate awaited those who were here cast on a strange shore like the scattered fragments of a wreck that has been the dreadful sport of the waves. Tears of pity dimmed her eyes. Her senses forsook her. When, holding her bundle of clothing in her hand, she felt her feet standing on solid ground, she knew not how she had got off the ship.

Catherine said nothing, but in her inmost heart she cried out again and again: "God be praised!"

CHAPTER III

The setting sun, which hung over the forest sea of Canada Creek, poured its purple beams over the travelers. They had just emerged from the woods through which they had been going the whole day by solitary, narrow Indian trails. At their feet lay the valley, filled with roseate evening mist, following the windings of the creek.

Lambert stopped the strong-limbed horse which he was leading by the bridle as they were ascending the valley, and said to his companion:

"This is Canada Creek, and that is our house."

"Where?" asked Catherine.

Leaning over the saddle and protecting her eyes from the sun with her hand she eagerly looked in the direction which the young man had indicated.

"There," said he, "toward the north, where the creek appears. Do you see it?"

"Now I do," said Catherine.

At this moment the horse, with expanded nostrils, snorted, and suddenly leapt sideways. The unprepared rider lost her balance and would have fallen off had not her companion, by a quick spring, caught her in his arms.

"It is nothing," said he, as she slid down to the

ground. "Old Hans acts as if he had never before
seen a snake. Are you not ashamed of yourself, old
fellow? So—keep quiet, so!" He patted the frightened horse on his short, thick neck, stripped off the
bridle and tied him to a sapling.

"You must have been terribly frightened," said he.
His voice and hands shook while he buckled on the
pillion which had become displaced.

"Oh, no," said Catherine.

She had seated herself on the root of a tree, and
looked over the valley where now, over the luxuriant
meadow which followed the course of the stream, a
fog began to rise. Yonder the sun was just dipping
into the emerald, forest sea, and the golden flames
on the trunks, boughs and tops of the great trees
were gradually fading away.

From above, the cloudless, greenish-blue evening
sky looked down, while a flock of wild swans was
flying northward up the valley. From time to time
they uttered their peculiar, melancholy cry, melodi-
ously softened by the distance. A deep, quiet stillness brooded over the primitive forest.

The young man stood leaning against the shoulder
of the horse. There rested on his brown face a deep,
sad anxiety. Often a shadow of restlessness and fear
passed over it, widely differing from the usual expression of the smooth, manly features, and obscuring the
light that commonly danced in the large blue eyes.
He looked now at the swans, which shone as silver

stars in the distant, rosy horizon—now at the maiden
who sat there, partly turned away from him. At
length, drawing a deep breath a couple of times, he
approached her.

"Catherine," said he.

She raised her handsome face. Her large brown
eyes were filled with tears.

"Are you sorry that you have come with me?" said
the young man.

Catherine shook her head.

"No," said she; "how unthankful I should then be."

"And yet, you are weeping."

"I am not weeping," said Catherine, as she drew
her hands across her eyes and tried to smile. "I was
just thinking how happy my father would have been,
had he, at the end of his wanderings, found this still
place. Ah! just so had he wished and dreamed.
Still it could not be so. How your parents will rejoice to see you again."

She was about to rise. Lambert touched her
shoulder.

"Stay yet a moment, Catherine, I have—I must
ask you something."

The anxiety that had already before showed itself
in his face become still greater. His brows were
contracted. His eyes had a stern, severe look.

Catherine looked up at him with astonishment.

"Had my parents meanwhile died and you and I,
Catherine, must dwell alone in yonder house—"

"You must not speak so, Lambert Sternberg," said
Catherine. "It is our duty to trust the Lord. They
are doubtless alive and well—they and your brother.
Why do we lose time? The evening is passing and
I am fully rested."

Lambert wished to make a reply, but the words
refused to pass his lips. He stared before him as if
in uncertainty, and at length turned to the horse, and
with a degree of violence thrust the bit between his
teeth. Then he threw the rifle, which stood leaning
against the trunk of a tree, on his shoulder and, leading his horse by the bridle, began to descend the
rocky declivity. Silently Catherine followed, carefully looking where she could with confidence set her
foot, casting many a glance at those going before.
The path was very steep and the horse often slid.
Lambert needed all his strength and carefulness, and
it was manifest that he did not once look back, nor
did he ask Catherine how she was getting along.
Meanwhile Catherine's heart palpitated. It seemed
as though the restlessness, the anxiety about his
home that spoke in Lambert's words and looks, had
also seized her. "Were they indeed dead—were they
all dead—and were we two, he and I, to dwell in
yonder house!"

They had reached the valley. Here, along the
creek, which flowed in many windings between the
meadow banks, there was an easier though narrower
path. The horse thrust forward his ears, neighed

and stepped along quicker.   Lambert had to hold him
by the bridle.   Catherine walked a little to one side.
It did not tire the slim, vigorous girl to come along.
It was not the exertion that caused her to breathe
with difficulty.   The silence which Lambert had not
broken for a long time pressed upon her more and
more.   She was not accustomed to it.   On the other
hand—this she now for the first time thought of—he
had toyed with her during the journey of weeks, he
had always talked with her in a way so kind and
good.   Now, however, in view of his nearer responsi-
bilities he had become silent.   He did not speak of
those belonging to him.   Indeed she would not have
known that his parents were living had he not, when
she asked him whether he thought that his mother
would be satisfied with her, replied that she should
give herself no uneasiness on that account.   Had he
not even now expressed a fear that he should not find
his parents alive?

"The kind man," said she to herself, "did not wish
to make the heart of the poor orphan heavy by tell-
ing me about his parents, and now he cannot wait
for the time of meeting them."

"Catherine," said he at that moment.

"Lambert," replied she, coming to his side, glad
that he had at last broken silence.   As he said no
more to her as she waited, she added, "You wished to
say something?"

"We shall not live there alone," indicating the

block-house with his eyes, standing but a few steps from them.

"No, surely not," she replied.

He gave her an unusual look.

"Do not be so anxious, kind Lambert, we are in God's care."

"No, certainly not," replied he.

He had not observed what she had last said, and only recalled her former words. But it affected her painfully when, through misapprehension, she had heard denied that which she believed, with all her heart, as her old father had believed in all need and trouble. "We are in God's care!" That was the text of his last sermon which, already himself dying, he had delivered between decks to his unhappy fellow sufferers. That was his last word as, a few hours later, he breathed out, in their arms, his pure spirit. Did not her pious childhood-faith approve itself to her in a wonderful manner? When all human help seemed impossible, did not a kind man, God-sent, come, and with a strong hand lead her out of the labyrinth, and carefully conduct her over hills and mountains, creeks and rivers, through endless forests and immeasurable prairies? Never, never, by the side of the good and strong one, had there come to her a feeling of anxiety or fear. Now, as she was nearing the end of her pilgrimage, should doubt find sly entrance? "I will protect and help you as a brother does his sister!" Had he promised too much?

Why did he walk so self-absorbed, so still and dumb at her side, now that he was so near his own hearth and that of his parents? Did he, perhaps, fear that he would not be kindly received on account of the stranger he was bringing home? Why was the house there before them so still? No barking of dogs. No sign of those who at the next moment might be expected to rush into the arms of the home-comer. The solitary house on the little hillock, gently descending from it on all sides, and standing near the creek which, like a snake through the grass, was quietly winding among the rushes, was perfectly silent. Silent and still were the dark woods which here and there overlooked the valley from the heights along the shore.

As she now reached the house Catherine felt as though her heart would leap forth as she observed that the lower story, built of immense logs, had no windows but narrow slits like the portholes in the walls of a fortress, and that the upper story was surrounded by a low, massive breastwork, and that the shingle roof was quite high. Lambert tied the horse to a heavy ring which was near the door, cast searching glances about the house and surroundings, murmured something that she did not understand, and finally pushed slowly against the heavy door which opened inward.

He disappeared in the house, came out after a few moments and said: "There is nobody here. We are entirely alone. Will you go with me?"

They were the very same words that he had addressed to her on the deck of the emigrant ship, and she again answered him as then:

"I will go with you, Lambert Sternberg."

She grasped the hand which he had extended to her and followed him into the forsaken house.

CHAPTER IV

While Lambert had been engaged within there came through the door a bright light, which Catherine now saw was produced by a large pine fagot burning in a corner of the room near a great stone-hearth. The room was half kitchen and store-room, and half living-room—such as the young woman had become acquainted with in many a farm-house where she had rested during her journey. It was fitted up with various utensils hanging on the walls and ceiling, standing in corners and lying on the floor. Near the hearth there were a couple of rough pine chairs, and, against the wall, a large four-cornered table, serving both for a dressing-table and for meals. There still stood on it a couple of earthen dishes on which were the remains of a meal to which a bear's ham, which had not again been hung upon its hook, contributed the principal part. The entire arrangement was planned on the basis of the simplest necessity. There was no trace of an endeavor after grace and beauty, or the merely agreeable. This observation, that the young maiden made with her first glance about the room, fell upon her heart even more heavily than the empty house. The house would fill up when the absent ones returned, but would she be happy in the company of those who lived here, who called it their home?

"I must look after my horse," said Lambert, "and after the rest of the things. You may meanwhile prepare the evening meal—you will probably find something. We will after that consider your sleeping apartment. It looks very bad here, but Conrad knows nothing about order. However, you can have a chamber upstairs. I will sleep below. I shall not go far, and will soon be back. Do not be afraid."

He said all this forcibly, in snatches, while prying into the corners, so that she scarcely understood him. Then he quickly left the house, and she heard him outside untie the horse and go away with it.

"Do not be afraid! Should I be so it would not be strange. How wonderful it all is! But he has been so heavenly kind to me, a poor girl; and surely his intentions are as honorable and true as ever. Where can they be? They must certainly be at some neighbor's." She had seen at a distance from the creek a couple of roofs. "Does he still expect them back? Now I will do what becomes a good maid who expects her master. What shall I begin with? Yes, that is it. So, it will soon begin to look more cheerful."

She turned to the hearth and in a few minutes had made a bright fire with the dry, prepared pine wood that lay near. Then she took from the hook the kettle that hung by a chain against the wall and filled it half full of water, which she drew from a pump that stood directly beside the hearth. She sought and soon found whatever else was needed for the preparation of the evening meal. She was uncertain of the number for whom she was to provide. She finally concluded that six would be the correct number: Lambert's parents, his brother Conrad, of whom he had spoken a couple of times, Lambert himself, and perhaps there might be another member of the family, or they might bring a guest with them. When she had finished this work she began to put the room in order, but only what would come right with but little labor. "For," said she, "I have no right to do it, and they might be displeased with me."

She had thus quietly labored for a quarter of an hour, and as there was for the moment nothing more to do and the water in the kettle was boiling, she went to the hearth and looked at the flaming fire, thinking that it must at least be time for Lambert to return. She heard a noise behind her. She turned half around and was greatly frightened when she saw, but a few steps from her, instead of Lambert, a stranger staring at her without moving, with a look of such wonder, as though he did not believe his own eyes. The light of the pine sticks burning with a bright flame fell full upon him. It was fortunate for Catherine that, the same moment, she saw that the giant-like man, clothed in a peculiar half-farmer, half-Indian garb, was quite young, and that his sunburned face was handsome, and that his great, wondering eyes had a merry look.

And now the young giant leaned his rifle, which he had allowed to slip to the floor, against the table, gave his strong hands a ringing slap, broke out in very loud laughter, threw himself into a chair which cracked in spite of its strong construction, sprang up again and approached the maiden, who drew back somewhat, again began to laugh, though not so loud, then was silent, shook his short, brown locks and said:

"Lambert has done this well; but where is the other one?"

Catherine did not answer. She did not know what to think of the words of the young man though they affected her disagreeably, and her heart began to beat powerfully.

The young giant looked about the room as though searching whether any one were hidden there. He then again directed his glances toward Catherine, but with a different expression in the large eyes which now shone with a deeper light. He said through his white teeth:

"You are handsome, girl. I have never before seen anything so beautiful. What is your name?"

"Catherine," said the young maiden, who felt that she must say something. "Catherine Weise. You are Conrad, Lambert's brother. I see it by the resemblance. Your brother Lambert has been very kind to me—very kind. We have just arrived. He

has gone to put the horse in the stable.   I think he
will soon be here.   You should have met him.   Will
the others also come soon?"

"Who should come?" asked Conrad.

"Your parents," said Catherine.   She said it very
faintly, fear, increasing every moment, almost stran-
gling her.

Conrad showed his white teeth.   "Our parents!"
cried he, "our parents!   They are long since dead.
You must be satisfied with us two."

"I will look for Lambert," said Catherine, and
tried to pass Conrad to the door.   Conrad stepped in
her way.

"So," said he smiling provokingly, "then Lambert
has brought you along for himself, the cunning fellow
—and I must look further.   Now, as for myself, I
am the younger man and can wait a little; but one kiss,
beautiful sister-in-law, that you must give me—that
is the least."

He stretched out his powerful hands and with giant
strength insolently drew the resisting girl to him and
kissed her glowing cheeks.

At this moment the water, which for a long time
had simmered, noisily, sissing and whizzing, poured
over the edge of the kettle in a large swell into the
fire which it almost extinguished.   A thick, gray
vapor, through which the light of the fire looked red,
rose and filled the room.   Catherine tore herself loose,
or was torn loose, she could not tell which; but there

were now two persons there struggling together, and
the other might well be Lambert.   She also thought
she had heard Lambert call her name, and so again,
as outside the evening wind fanned her cheeks glowing with anger and shame.

Within, the vapor had disappeared.   Conrad, having disengaged himself with a powerful effort from his
assailant, fell laughing on his neck.

"Lambert, dear, best Lambert!"

"Let me go!" said Lambert, freeing himself from
the embrace.   "Let me go.   Catherine!"

He looked with wandering, anxious eyes about the
poorly lighted room.

"She has gone out," said Conrad.   "I will bring
her again for you."

"No, no, *I* will, I must," called Lambert, already at
the door.   "At least take me along—I beg you, Conrad, let me.   I will afterwards explain everything to
you.   Catherine!   For the mercy of God!   She may
have fallen into the creek!"

"Stupid stuff!" said Conrad, who, less excited than
his brother, had cast his eyes, sharp as those of a
falcon, in every direction.   "There she sits, there,
do you see?"

"I will go to her alone."

"You may, so far as I am concerned.   And Lambert, listen, have you not also brought me a wife?"

But Lambert was already hastening with beating
heart to the place where he saw Catherine sit, or lie,

he could not tell which, on account of the distance
and the evening twilight which now prevailed.

Catherine had run straight forward from the hill on
which the house stood until she saw the creek at her
feet. She now ran along its edge, scarcely knowing
what she wished to do, or whither to go, driven by
the painful feeling that the man whom she had trusted
as she did her God, had deceived her. She could
not make it clear to herself. Everything had come so
quickly—had passed like a shadow in the smoke and
mist from the fire on the hearth. What she had con-
ceived to be a family, consisted of two brothers fighting with each other—fighting on her account. And
this was the end of her long pilgrimage, which she
had begun in such a hopeful spirit—with a constantly
increasing confidence—yes, at last with wonderful
joyfulness. This the end! "O, my God, my God!"
groaned the young girl, stopping and looking anxiously into the wilderness which in fearful silence surrounded her, the night with its gathering darkness
settling down upon her. "O, my God, my God!"

A bridge, consisting of an immense tree trunk, led
across the creek at the place where she now was.
She had already set one foot on the dangerous cross-
ing when it suddenly became dark before her eyes.
Involuntarily she turned and sank back on her knees,
laying her head against the trunk of the tree. Her
senses forsook her.

Then, as if from a great distance, she heard her

name called, "Catherine!" Again, but now quite
near, "Catherine!" She opened her eyes. Near her
in the grass kneeled Lambert. He had seized her
powerless hands. His long, smooth, brown hair fluttered confusedly in the evening wind about his pale,
anxious face.

"Catherine," he said again, "can you forgive me?"
She looked at him. She wished to say: "Why
have you done this to me?" But her heart was too
full. Two large tears rolled down her cheeks. Others
followed them unrestrained. She wished to withdraw
her hands from those of Lambert. He, however, in
his desperation, held her fast, and in a despairing
voice, cried: "For God's sake, Catherine, listen to
me. I meant it well. I wanted to tell you a hundred
times, but I could not. I thought you would not so
willingly go with me if you knew the actual state of
things. I endured a great fear, as you may have perceived, when we passed through Albany and Schenectady and the valley of the Mohawk, where they all
know me. I always went first into the houses to
beg the people not to speak to you of my situation.
To-day I left the road and came on through the
woods so that nobody here on the creek should meet
me. It was not right; it was very foolish; it was
bad in me that I did not requite your confidence with
confidence on my part; but I did not know how to
help myself. For God's sake, forgive me, Catherine."
She had now withdrawn her hands and laid them

across her breast. Lambert had risen. He brushed his hair from his face. With all the thoughts that crossed his brain, with all the feelings that filled his breast, he knew not what more he should say—what he had said.

"Catherine, believe me, oh, believe me! I had not thought when I reached New York that I should not return alone to my home. I will take you back again —will take you where you will. My uncle Christian Ditmar and his wife, my aunt, are old and childless and will be glad to have you; and Conrad and I will again live as we have hitherto. Conrad has ever been to me a kind and faithful brother, and he now feels very sorry that he has so offended you. We will both watch over you—watch over you all—as we always have here where we are the farthest settlers. However, as you will, Catherine, as you will."

She had now raised herself up, and, as she stood there in the light of the moon which had for some time risen above the edge of the forest, Lambert thought that the beloved maiden had never before appeared so beautiful.

She had folded her hands, and, not looking at Lambert, but upward, she said softly but firmly: "I will go with you, Lambert Sternberg—come what will."

They walked back toward the house, side by side, the moon shining in the deep blue sky with radiant clearness. From time to time Lambert cast sly glances at the beloved one. He had yet so much to tell her—so very much—but he would not speak since she herself was silent, and he knew that she could speak more beautifully than he had ever heard any one speak before. It was also so well and he was so thankful that at last the burden was lifted from his soul, and that she had forgiven him and would entirely forgive him when she learned how much he had suffered.

This Catherine had already perceived in the painful vehemence of a man otherwise so quiet and self-contained. She had felt it in the storm that had swept through her own soul. Now after the turmoil of the storm she was at peace. What had happened? Was everything that she silently hoped, lived upon, cherished, forever destroyed? Or, amid thunder-claps, did a new world bloom far more beautiful than she had ever dreamed?

Thus, lost in their own peculiar thoughts, they again reached the house.

"Do you come at last?" said Conrad.

He was standing in the door which he now opened wide for the two. Then he gave his hand to Catherine and his brother and greeted them for the first time. "You before took me so by surprise," said he, "that I did not know where my head stood. In what a confusion everything about here lay! It had become somewhat disordered during the two months that you, Lambert, was away. You know I do not well understand housekeeping. I came home a couple

of hours ago, having been upon Black River for eight
days after beaver. However, instead of beaver I
found Onandagas, whose manner was far from friendly
—the cursed scoundrels. I went to Uncle Ditmar's
who had, meanwhile, kept our cows. Bless has
calved. Ditmar will keep the calf if you do not wish
to raise it. Take seats here. I have meanwhile re-
arranged the evening meal as well as I could after my
awkward interference. There is baked ham, your
favorite dish, Lambert."

Conrad was unusually busy while he thus spoke.
He set the chairs to the table, pulled them back, that
he might wipe them off with his brown hand, and
then set them up again. Again and again he put
wood on the fire, so that the fire crackled and the
flame went roaring up the chimney. For no definite
reason, except that it had to be so, he kicked his wolf-
hound, Pluto, while she, having just come in, kept
blinking at Catherine with her large yellow eyes. He
himself did not look at the strange girl, and when
his glance accidentally passed over her face he became red and embarrassed, and speedily turned his
eyes away again.

In this way he acted during the whole meal. He
talked, stood up, sat down again, tried to put things
in order, but brought them into greater confusion, so
that Lambert became red in the face and thanked the
Lord when he saw Catherine smiling in a friendly
way. She thought she could interpret Conrad's con-

duct in his favor.   It was apparent enough that it had
not made an unfavorable impression on the young
and beautiful girl.   It cost her no trouble now and
again to return a friendly word to his talk.   Lambert was astonished, and it sounded strange to him as
she once laughed in the same cheerful, soft tone in
which she spoke.   He had not heard her laugh once
during her whole journey.

So he sat there full of thankful joy that everything
had turned out so well after he had been very de-
spondent and was filled with secret unrest like one
who, having with difficulty escaped a great danger,
does not venture to yield to the feeling of security
and seems to feel the ground shaking under his feet.

But as the meal was now drawing to a close another care began to press upon him with increasing
weight.   During the journey, in the farm-houses
which they entered, which were often very small, it
had happened more than once that he had passed the
night in the same room with the family and his companion.   Two or three nights when they could reach
no human habitation they had taken their rest in the
forest, and he had seen the beloved maiden by the
light of the camp-fire sleeping peacefully, while he
looked up through the tops of the trees and thanked
God that he was permitted to watch over her slumber,
But this occurred on the journey—an unusual condition, which could not and should not last.   There was
in the upper story a store-room partitioned off, in

which one of the brothers used to sleep, while the
other had his simple couch in a small recess in the
lower room. The brothers had hit upon this arrangement the preceding year, when the inroads of the
French necessitated redoubled watchfulness. Afterwards, though the danger was over, they had kept
up the custom until Lambert's departure. Lambert
had thought of each room for Catherine, but Conrad
had mentioned during the meal that, on his eight-
days' excursion, he had learned that the French were
stirring again. Consequently renewed watchfulness
was necessary, and that since Lambert must be very
tired from his journey, he would undertake the watch
for that night.

"Then we will in turn both watch above," said
Lambert after a pause. "Catherine will be satisfied
for the night here below. To-morrow we will make
a better arrangement for her. Is that satisfactory,
Catherine?"

"Quite so," replied the young woman. "I saw in
the recess sweet-smelling hay, and here is the beautiful white bear-skin; do not trouble yourselves. I
shall get along all right. Good night."

She gave Lambert her hand and then Conrad, who
looked on with surprise. He wondered at his brother,
and followed him up the narrow stairway after they
had bolted and barricaded the door.

Catherine watched them as they ascended, drew a
deep breath, passed her hand over her forehead, and

began to clear away the supper table, and to wash up
and put away the dishes, that she might with better
courage carry forward the work of reducing things to
order which she had before timidly begun.   This took
a long time.   Often she stood benumbed in the midst
of her work with her hand pressed against her forehead.   Her heart was so full she could have sat down
and shed a flood of tears.   At the same time a firm,
unchecked serenity filled her soul, such as she had
experienced when quite a young thing playing at for-
feits when the band of children in their colored dresses
wildly pursued each other.

Then awakened out of such strange dreams, she
again quietly continued her work, and at last looked
about the room with a self-satisfied air, since it had
now assumed quite a different appearance.   Having
carefully put out the fire on the hearth, she sought
her modest couch that she had prepared in the recess
on the farther side of the large room.

Through the narrow port-holes in the thick plank
wall there stole in streaks of the moon's rays, spreading about her a faint twilight.   It was easy to breathe
in the fresh forest exhalation which blew in at the
openings and played about her cheeks.   The brook
purled uninterruptedly.   From time to time there
was a rustle, first gentle, then swelling out, and then
again holding back like the tones of an organ.   It
was the solemn music of the primitive forest.   She
had already noticed this music on her journey when,

sleeping under the trees on gathered moss, she, with dream-veiled, half-open eyes, saw Lambert sitting at the camp-fire. She could now also hear his step as he made the round of the gallery above. Conrad's tread would be heavier. Once he stopped directly over her head. Was he looking in the distance for the blood-thirsty enemies? or was he listening to the mocking-bird's wonderful song which she had for some time noticed coming from the forest in soft, sobbing tones, as the nightingale had warbled, over in her German home, in the linden tree at the gable of the parsonage. Then again it.shrieked like a vex-atious parrot, or laughed like a magpie. This sounded quite ludicrous. Then it was no more the mocking-bird's twofold, demon-like singing, but two human voices, and Lambert spoke in excited, suffering tones: "Catherine, can you forgive me?" and Conrad laughed, saying: "Catherine is not at all angry," and she had to smile, and with a smile on her lips she fell asleep.

Meanwhile, as Catherine had correctly supposed, Lambert, walking slowly over the floor of the gallery, kept watch, though Conrad, recurring to what he had reported, assured him that, for the present, the dan-ger of which he had before spoken did not exist, and that he had only mentioned it that he might have good grounds for leaving. He then became very an-gry as Lambert replied, "I do not know what you mean," threw himself on the bed in the watch-chamber and declared that he was too tired to say another word.

However he did not sleep, for as Lambert, after an hour, softly walked past the open door of the watch-chamber, he thought he heard his name spoken. He stopped and looked in.

"Did you call me, Conrad?"

"Yes," replied Conrad, who had raised himself on his elbow, "I wished to ask you something."

"What?"

"Are you then not married?"

"No; why?"

"Oh! I only asked; so good night."

"Conrad, dear Conrad, I wish with all my heart to tell you everything." But Conrad had already sunk back on the bear skin and had fallen asleep, or pretended that he had.

Lambert went sadly out. "To-morrow," said he to himself, "before we see Catherine, he shall know it, and he will help me, and all will be well."

CHAPTER V

Lambert, having, in the early morning, lain down by the side of Conrad, awoke late and found his brother gone. He had left the block-house at sunrise. Catherine was up and occupied about the hearth when Conrad lightly descended the stairs. He was in a great hurry, and declined the morning soup which she offered him. He would certainly be back before night. Then he took his rifle, hung about him his game bag, and, with Pluto at his heels, went up the creek with long strides.

"The wild youth," said Lambert.

He was quite displeased with Conrad, but that he had intentionally avoided him did not enter his mind. Conrad had acted strangely enough last evening, but then the older brother was accustomed to the unreliable, crisp and often silly humors of the younger one. "Why should Conrad give up a hunt to-day which perhaps he had prearranged with his companions? He will doubtless return by noon with a fat deer and a woodman's appetite."

So said Lambert while, standing at the hearth, he partook of his morning meal. However he did not say that, on the whole, he was not so much put out by his brother's absence—that he reluctantly gave up the sweet habit of being alone with Catherine that he might talk freely with her.

But this morning the pleasant conversation was wanting. Catherine was still and, as Lambert now saw, was pale, and her beaming, brown eyes were veiled. Now that the end of her journey had been reached she felt how great the strain had been; but soon, smiling, accommodated herself to the situation.

"You need not feel concerned," said she. "In a couple of days—perhaps hours—all will be regained. I will not boast, but I have always been able to accomplish what others could, and often a little more, and, if you are not too strict a master, you shall be satisfied with your maid-servant."

To Lambert it seemed as if the sun had suddenly been overcast. With trembling hand he put down the cup which he had not yet entirely emptied.

"You are not my maid-servant, Catherine," he said gently.

"Yes I am, Lambert, yes I am, though you magnanimously tore up the evidence of my indebtedness," replied the young maiden. "I owe you none the less on that account. The debt is now doubled. You know it well and yet it is proper for me to say it. I desired to be to you a good and faithful maid-servant—to you and yours. I supposed nothing else but that your parents were still alive, and I heartily rejoiced that I could serve them. You said nothing about your parents, I think, because you did not wish to make me feel sad. Now your parents, like mine, are dead, and you live here alone with your brother, so I am your maid-servant and your brother's."

Lambert made a motion as though he wished to reply, but his half-raised arm fell powerless, and his opened lips again closed. He had intended to say: "I love you, Catherine. Do you not see it?" How could he now say it?

Catherine continued:

"I beg you, Lambert, with this understanding, to talk with your brother, if you have not already done so. You are the elder and know me better. He is young and impetuous, as it seems, and now sees me for the first time. And now, Lambert, you surely have something better to do than to stand here and talk with me. I have to clear away a little here yet, and will follow you should you not go far, if you do not object. I should like to see all, and know about every part."

She turned to him and gave him her hand. "Does that please you?" she asked smiling.

"Entirely, entirely," replied Lambert. Tears stood in his eyes, but the dear girl wanted it so, and that was enough.

"I will first go to the barn-yard," said he, "and then into the forest. This afternoon I intended to go to Uncle Ditmar's. Perhaps you will accompany me."

He went out hastily. Catherine looked at him with sad smiles. "You good, dear, best man," said she, "it is not my fault that I distress you, but I must think of us all. The madcap will probably now be satisfied."

Catherine now felt herself somewhat relieved of the weight that had lain on her heart since the peculiar scene with Conrad in the morning. Involuntarily she constantly thought about how alarmed Conrad appeared when, as he came down the narrow, steep stairs, he found her already on the hearth; how he had then approached her and stared at her with his large, glistening eyes, and had said: "Are you man and wife, or are you not? If you are, then it will be best for me to send a bullet through my head; but, lie not—for God's sake, do not lie, otherwise I will indeed shoot myself, but first surely both of you."

Then as Catherine drew back from the violence, he began to laugh. "Now, one does not lightly shoot such a brother dead, who is so good that he could not be better, and a girl who is so handsome, so wonderfully beautiful. So far as I am concerned I need feel no anxiety about being shot dead. This can happen to me any day. Pluto, beast, are you again staring at her? Wait! I will teach you manners." With this he hastened away. Outside Pluto howled grievously, as though she would teach Catherine that her master was not accustomed to indulge in vain threats.

"Now he will be satisfied," said Catherine, yet a couple of times, while she cleared away the breakfast and made some preparations for the simple dinner.

To-day she did not, like yesterday, have to gather up
laboriously what she needed; everything was at her
hand. Everything appeared as if familiar to her—as
though she had known it from youth up. She hum-
med her favorite song, "Were I a wild falcon I would
soar aloft," and then interrupted herself and said:
"It has been childish for me to be so fearful. He
loves him; that one sees clearly. He has called him
the best brother, and surely, at the bottom of his
heart, he is kind though his eyes have so wild a look.
Before glittering eyes which are so handsome one
needs not be afraid. But Lambert's eyes are still
handsomer."

Catherine stepped to the door. It was a most
beautiful spring morning. Small white clouds passed
quietly over the light blue sky. Golden stars danced
in the creek. Dew-drops sparkled in the luxuriant
grass of the meadow—here in emerald green, in blue
and purple shades there. The woods which encircled
the hill on which the house stood looked down quietly.
Over a rocky height that projected steep out of the
forest there hovered a great eagle with extended
wings sporting in the balmy air that was breathing
through the valley and whose every puff was charged
with balsamic aroma.

Catherine folded her hands and her eyes filled with
tears. It seemed to her as if she were again standing
in the small church of her home village, and that she
heard her father's mild voice pronounce the benedic-

tion over the congregation: "The Lord let the light of His countenance fall upon you and give you peace."

The last remains of unrest had passed away from her and, in her present mood, she went to seek Lambert, whom she supposed to be at the buildings which, as she passed around the block-house, she saw standing at some distance towards the forest.

She found him working at a hedge which inclosed part of a field in which the lance-shaped, bright leaves of the Indian-corn waved in the morning wind. Young, red-blossomed apple trees, whose trunks had been carefully wound with thorns, had been planted around the fields.

"This the deer did last night," said Lambert, as he approached a damaged place. "Here are the fresh tracks. Conrad knows how to keep them respectful, but during the eight days that he has been away they have again become bold."

"I will help you," said Catherine, after she had looked on for a few miuntes.

'This is no labor for you," said Lambert, looking up.

"So, once for all, you must not speak," serenely replied Catherine. "If you want a princess in your house you must at once send me away again. I own myself unfit for that."

Lambert smiled with pleasure when he saw how skillfully she took hold of the matter, and how handy she was. He now noticed for the first time that

the roses had again blossomed on her cheeks; and as
she now, in helping him, bent over and back, the
agreeable play of the lines of her slender, girlish body
filled him with trembling delight.

"But you also should not be unemployed," said
Catherine.

The young man, blushing deeply, returned to his
work with redoubled zeal, so that it was soon completed.

"What comes next?" asked Catherine.

"I intended to go up into the woods to look after
my pine trees. There will be probably more to do
there than here, where my kind uncle has kept every
thing so well in order. But about woodcraft he understands little or nothing; and Conrad concerns
himself only with his hunting. It was fortunate that
I could do the chief labor before I left home in the
spring."

He hung the gun, which leaned against the hedge
near him, over his shoulder and looked at Catherine.

Lingering he said: "Will you go with me? It is
not far."

"That is truly fortunate," said Catherine. "You
know I am shy of long roads. Will you not rather
saddle Hans?"

She called the horse, grazing in an enclosure near
by, in which there was also a small flock of black-
wooled sheep. He pricked up his ears, came slowly,
swinging his tail, and put his head over the bars.

"You good Hans," said Catherine, brushing the thick forelock out of the eyes of the animal, "I gave you a good deal of trouble on the long journey."

"The trouble was not so very great. Is it not so, old Hans?" said Lambert.

Hans seemed to think that to such an idle question no answer was necessary and went on quietly chewing his last mouthful of grass. The young people stood and looked on and stroked the head and neck of the animal, while in the branches of a blossoming apple tree a robin-redbreast sang. Their hands touched. Lambert's large eyes assumed a determined expression and then were raised with a cordial look to the blushing face of the maiden.

"Now you must also show me the barn-yard," said Catherine.

"Cheerfully," said Lambert.

They entered the barn-yard which like the house was inclosed with a stone-wall of the height of a man, and contained several low buildings formed of logs. First the stable in which, in the winter and in bad weather, Hans, the cows and the sheep stayed quietly together. This was now empty with the exception of a couple of half-grown pigs grunting within a partition, and a large flock of hens and turkeys which had been contentedly scratching in the straw, but now, frightened at the unwelcome intrusion, cackling and flying apart rushed out of the open door. Then they entered the work-shop, in which Lambert worked during the winter, and where, besides excellent timber and all kinds of tools, there were standing, begun and finished, tubs which would have done credit to a cooper.

"In the fall these are all filled with tar and rosin," said Lambert, "and sent to Albany. It won't be long before I must stick to this, and my Uncle Ditmar, of whom I learned coopering, will help me, I suppose, and also Conrad, though he does not like mechanical labor. Still he can do anything he pleases, and does it better than one who devotes his life to it."

Catherine was pleased to hear that Lambert was so proud of his younger brother, but did not speak of it. It seemed to her as if a dark shadow had passed over her heart, which had but now been as sunny as the surrounding golden, spring landscape.

They left the barn-yard and, ascending by degrees, soon reached the edge of the woods, which here extended back farther from the level ground, so that, as they turned about, the valley lay like a great meadow in the woods, in the midst of which was the blockhouse on the hill. The creek was concealed by the reeds which fringed its shore. Deep peace rested in happy quietude on the earth in its morning freshness. But up in the air there appeared an unusual spectacle. The eagle which Catherine had before observed had been joined by another. They sailed directly over the house and wound their circles together swifter and ever swifter until, with loud outcries, they rushed against each other, striking with their mighty wings, whirling round each other, clasping each other, and falling like a stone. Then again they separated, sailed aloft, again rushed together, until at length one flew toward the woods followed by the other.

"A hateful sight," said Catherine. "The angry beasts!"

"We are accustomed to that," said Lambert.

Catherine was greatly disturbed by this battle scene. Involuntarily she had again to think of Conrad.

As they now turned into the woods she asked:

"Do you truly love your brother?"

"And he me," said Lambert.

"He is yet so young," Catherine began again.

"Ten years younger than I. I am thirty-two. Our mother died when he was born. Good Aunt Ditmar, our sainted mother's sister, took him home since my father and I, poor youngster, naturally did not know how to help ourselves. When he was a couple of years old he came again to us, though his aunt would gladly have kept him. But father did not stand any too well with uncle, and was jealous, fearing that his child would become entirely estranged from him. So I waited on and brought up the little orphaned rogue as best I could, and, since he grew so, I thought that any mother would be proud of the boy. Then, when I could no longer carry him, I played with him, and taught him the little I had learned, and so we have been together day and night, and an angry word has never passed between us, though he was as wild and intractable as a young bear. Father's position in respect to him was very difficult, being himself a determined man and quite passionate. Once, being at variance, father raised his hand against the eleven-year-old boy, who was as brave and proud as a man. He ran away into the woods and did not return, so that we thought that he had either committed suicide, or had been torn in pieces by the bears. Meanwhile my young gentleman stuck among the Indians at Oneida Lake and did not let anything be seen or heard of him for three years, until, a few days after father's death, he suddenly entered the block-house where I sat alone and sad. At first I did not know him, for he had grown a couple of heads taller and was dressed in Indian style. But he fell upon my neck and wept bitterly, and said:

" 'I heard by chance that our father was lying on his death-bed. I have been walking three days and three nights to see him again.' In the midst of his weeping he threw back his head and, with sparkling eyes, exclaimed: 'But do not think that I have forgiven him for striking me; but I am sorry that I ran away.' So he came again as he had gone, wild and proud, and at the next moment soft and kind."

Lambert was silent. After a short pause he said:

"I wish I had told you all this before; you would then not have been so frightened last evening."

"And this morning," said Catherine to herself.

Lambert continued: "They here call him the Indian, and the name fits him in more than one respect. At least no Indian would undertake to compete with him in those things in which they chiefly excel. In all their arts Conrad beats them; and then he loves the hunt, the forest and rambling ways just as the red-skins do. But his heart is true as pure gold, and in that he is not a red-skin, who are all as false as a jack-o'-lantern in the swamp. For this reason we all here on the Mohawk and on the Schoharie, old and young, love him. Wherever there are German settlers there he comes on his hunting expeditions, and is everywhere welcome. The people sleep without fear when he is there, for they know they are guarded by the best rifle in the colony."

Lambert's eyes brightened as he spoke about his brother. Suddenly his face became beclouded.

"Who knows," continued he, "how different it might have been last year had he been here with us? But when Belletre broke loose with his devilish Indians and his French, who are much worse devils, we were entirely unprepared. We would not believe the Indian who brought us the news. Conrad would have known what there was of it, and would soon have brought it out. But he remained above between the lakes on a hunt; so we missed his arm and rifle. Then took place the remarkable circumstance that they did not come here to Canada Creek, and that our houses escaped their ravages. This afterward caused bad blood, and one could hear whisperings about treachery, though, at the first alarm, we all hurried forward and did our share. Conrad helped us fight in his own way. He says nothing about it, but I think that many an Indian, who in the morning went hunting, was vainly waited for at his camp-fire in the evening, and has not to this day returned to his wigwam."

A shudder passed over Catherine. What had the wild man said this morning? "As far as it concerns me I need not trouble myself about being shot to death." Dreadful! Had she not seen as she came up the Mohawk valley where many houses had been burned which had not been rebuilt, the entire families having been killed by the merciless enemies? And how many plain wooden crosses in green fields, along the road, in the edge of the woods, where a peaceful farmer, a helpless wife, a playful child, had been pitilessly killed. No, no! It was an honorable conflict for house and home, for body and life—the same conflict through which her good father with his whole congregation had been driven out of Germany. They knew not how to resist their shameless and disorderly oppressors except by flight over the sea into this wilderness at the furthest west. Whither shall they yet fly, since the same enemy even here begrudges them life and freedom? Here one cannot say: "Let us forsake our houses and shake the dust from our feet." Here the word is wait, fight, conquer, or die. Not in empty threatening did the farmer as he went to his peaceful labor carry his gun on his shoulder.

"I wish I too knew how to handle the rifle," said Catherine.

"Like my Aunt Ursul," said Lambert laughing. "She shoots as well as any one of us, Conrad naturally being excepted. Nor does she leave her rifle at home. Here we are, at the pinery."

They had reached a tall forest, such as Catherine on her journey, had not hitherto seen. The powerful trunks shot up like the pillars of a dome and intertwined their mighty tops in an arch through whose dark vaults here and there red sun-rays flashed. The morning wind soughed through the wide halls, having now become stronger, and ascending, gently died at the top like the murmur of the sea.

"This seems to have stood so since the first day of creation," said Catherine.

"And yet its days are numbered," said Lambert. "In a couple of years there will be little more to be seen of it. I am sorry for the beautiful trees, and now, since you so admire them, I am doubly sorry. But there is no longer any remedy. See, here my labor begins."

A slight depression, through which a brooklet purled on its way to the creek, separated this piece of woods from another which had already been prepared the second year for the manufacture of tar.

Lambert explained to his companion that each of the large trees was divided into four quarters. "In the spring, as soon as the sap begins to rise, the north quarter, where the sun has the least power, is peeled off for two feet in order to draw off the turpentine. In the fall, before the sap begins to slacken, the southern quarter is treated in the same way. The following spring the eastern side, and in the fall the western side, is in like manner peeled. Then the upper part of the tree, filled with turpentine, is cut down and split up and roasted in an oven so prepared as to secure the tar. This I will show you later. This indeed is not a pleasing sight," said Lambert, "nor will I take you farther, where the poor naked stumps stand and decay. It cannot well be otherwise. One must live, and we here on Canada Creek have nothing else, or scarcely anything else, since our small cultivated acreage must be devoted to our most urgent necessities. So must also our live stock, though we have plenty of fertile plow-land and rich meadow-land. But what can one do when he is every instant in danger, and his crops are destroyed, and his herds are driven off? They must leave us our pine trees, and our ovens can soon be rebuilt. To replace the burnt casks and utensils we make new ones. Hence it was for us a question of life or death when, last winter, Mr. Albert Livingston wished to confine us to the valley, and claimed the woods on the hills for himself, notwithstanding that we had first bought both valley and forest from the Indians, and again after that from the Government. But all this I told you often enough on the journey, and you have listened patiently, and rejoice that the business has been arranged in our favor. God be praised—"

"And your faithful care," said Catherine. "You had it hard enough on the long, tiresome journey, from which you did not return unencumbered. After you had been relieved of the old care you were laden with a new one in me, a poor, helpless girl."

"Shall I deny it?" replied Lambert. "Yes, Catherine, with you there came a new care to me. You know what I mean. I feared I had done wrong to bring you here, where everybody's life is in daily, yes, hourly danger. This indeed I did not conceal from you, though I felt that you would not on this account be frightened back. But—"

"Then don't distress yourself further about it," said Catherine. "Or do you think you have been deceived in me?"

"No," answered Lambert. "But since we are here, it has appeared to me as though I should have set the matter forth more pressingly. So I also blame myself that I let Conrad go away this morning without first more fully ascertaining what he knows about the enemy. He is too careless to take to heart anything of that kind. I should use better judgment."

"Better judgment, but not less courage," said Catherine. "If I must believe that my coming has robbed you of your cool courage, how could I forgive myself for having come here with you? No, Lambert, you must not so wrong me. I will also learn to use the rifle like Ursul. Why do you laugh?"

"I cannot think of you and the good old lady together without laughing," said Lambert.

"Perhaps I shall also live to be old, and, it is to be hoped, good. I shall then take it amiss if mischievous young people laugh at me."

"You old!" said Lambert, shaking his head. "You old! This I can conceive as little as how this rivulet must begin if it would flow up these rocks!"

They now went on between the tree-trunks down to the creek, and were walking along the edge where, in the mud of the shore, bison and deer had impressed their deep trails. The stream did not run as smoothly here as on the level ground. Its course was obstructed, now by rocks covered with moss a hundred years old, now by an immense tree-trunk which had fallen diagonally across, and whose withered branches stretched down into the brown water. A little further up it had to make its way over rocks, over which it leapt in indescribable, foam-covered cascades. From where they both stood one could see a part of the fall, like the fluttering ends of a white garment. The roar was softened by the distance and accorded remarkably well with the sound of the morning wind in the majestic tree-tops. With this exception there was an oppressive stillness in the primitive forest,

which the occasional flight of a flock of pigeons over-
head, the hammering of the woodpecker, the cawing
of crows, the chirping of a little bird high above in
the branches, and the piping of a little squirrel,
seemed to make only the stiller. Soft vaporous
shadows filled the woods. But in the clear space
above the creek there was spread a golden twilight
bewitchingly woven out of light and shadow. In this
enchanting light how bright the beloved one appeared
to her lover. He could not turn his eyes from her as
he now sat near her feet in the moss. Her rich, dark
hair which encircled her well-formed head like a
crown; the beautiful, slanting brows, the long, silky
eyelashes; the sweet face; the heavenly form—ah!
all this, on the long journey, had made a deep impression; but now it seemed as if he had not known
it before—as though he now saw for the first time
that she was so beautiful, so wonderfully beautiful.
Also her dark eyelashes were raised, and her glance
wandered over the blue eyes which had never before
seemed so deep and bright, turned back timidly, then
looked again more keenly, and could no longer withdraw themselves; then out of their blue depths there
came such wonderful flashes that her heart stood still,
and suddenly again she felt it bounding and beating
against the heart of the beloved man who held her
infolded in his arms. Then they released each other.
Each caught the other's hand. They sank again into
each other's arms, exchanged warm kisses and prom-

ises, and laughed, and cried, and said they had loved
each other from the moment in which they first saw
each other, and would do so to the last.

Suddenly Catherine shrunk back. "Conrad!" she
cried. "O, my God! Lambert, what are we beginning?"

"What has happened, my darling?" asked Lambert,
while he sought again to draw the beloved one to
him.

"No, no," said Catherine, "this must first be arranged. O, why did I not tell you? But how could
I speak of it before? Now indeed I must speak, even
though it be too late."

Without hesitating and in a becoming manner she
told Lambert what Conrad had said in the morning,
and how strange his conduct, and how threatening
his appearance had been. "I seem constantly to hear
his laugh," said she at last. "Great God, there he
is!"

She pointed with her trembling hand up the creek
to the place where, between the dark underwood, the
foam-streaks of the waterfall fluttered.

"Where?" asked Lambert.

"Conrad! I thought I saw him slipping away between the trunks of the trees."

Lambert shook his head.

"Then he would be there yet," said he. "It must
have been a deer that wanted to go to the spring.
Surely you are causelessly frightened. I can well

believe that the youth finds my beautiful girl handsome, but love as I do, that he cannot. Hereafter
he will be happy in seeing me happy."

"But now I surely have heard a human voice,"
cried Catherine.

"I, too, this time," said Lambert, "but it came from
up the creek. Hark!"

"He, holla, holla, he, ho!" it now sounded.

"That is Aunt Ursul," said Lambert. "How does
she come now to be here?"

A dark shadow passed over his face, which however at once disappeared as Catherine impressed a
hearty kiss on his lips, and said: "Quick, Lambert;
let us now go to meet your aunt. See that she ob-
serves nothing. Do you hear?"

"There she is already," said Lambert, half vexed,
half laughing, as now a large person, whose clothes
were an unusual mixture of women's and men's clothing, and who, carrying a rifle on her shoulder, pressing through the bushes, soon reached the pair.

CHAPTER VI

"So!" said Aunt Ursul. "There you are, sir!"

She remained standing, took her rifle from her shoulder and looked with large, round eyes on those who were approaching, like a beast of prey on a coming victim.

"God bless you, aunt," said Lambert, extending his hand to his old friend in salutation. "It is long since we have seen each other."

"And it might have been longer had it depended on you, sir," replied Aunt Ursul. "But one must first visit his pinery. Relatives and friends come later. It is fortunate that Aunt Ursul knows her people, or she might have had to look long for you, sir."

She threw her gun with a powerful swing on her shoulder, turned short on the heel of her man's boots, and began to stride back over the road along the creek by which she had come. She had returned Lambert's salutation but slightly, and had not noticed Catherine at all.

"How did you learn that I am back?" asked Lambert.

"Not from you, sir," replied Aunt Ursul.

"How is uncle?"

"As usual."

"You have taken such good care of my things—"

"One must, when the men are wandering about the country."

"You well know, aunt, that I did not remain so long away for release from labor, nor entirely on my own account. Nor was my journey useless. The business that took me to New York is so arranged that you and others will be satisfied."

"So!" said Ursul.

"And I have likewise brought with me for you a young female friend, whom you will love as she deserves, and whom you will receive kindly as you do all who need your help."

"So!" said Aunt Ursul.

The path was so narrow that two could not walk abreast. Ursul did not turn about, but Lambert now did so and observed that Catherine was quite pale, and that tears stood in her eyes. The sight cut him to the heart, as he had but a little before seen the beautiful face radiant with happiness. "Have good courage, my girl," said he softly. "She does not mean unkindly."

Catherine tried to smile through her tears, and bowed as if she would say: "Let it pass. Since you love me I can bear anything."

"Lambert!" called Ursul, who was vigorously walking on, "come here!"

"Only go," stammered Catherine; "but, for God's sake, tell her nothing. I could not endure it."

The young man tore himself away with a powerful effort and followed Ursul Ditmar, whom he soon overtook.

"Come to my side," said Aunt Ursul; "the path is wide enough so you need no longer trot behind me."

Lambert did as his aunt desired. Aunt Ursul could not bear opposition, and Lambert had from his youth honored her as a second mother. However he could not refrain from saying with mild reproach, "You are very rough with the poor girl, aunt."

"So!" said the dame. "Do you think so? It is naturally very important for an old person like me to know what such a look into the world means. No, I may as well tell you what I think. You have done a foolish thing, sir, do you hear—a besotted, foolish thing in that at such a time' you have burdened yourself with a woman. If, instead, you had brought half a dozen men, these we could indeed have used to better advantage."

"But, Aunt Ursul, first hear me—"

"I will not listen! I know the whole story as though I had been present from the beginning. Poor famished creatures, who all looked as though they had already for four weeks played the ghost. Surely! It is a sin and shame, and may the evil one pay back the greedy sharpers and Hollanders, and pour melted gold down their hungry throats! But when a gun is fired off it is well not to be in front of it.

Why did you stand near and gaze when you knew that you had such a butter-heart in your breast? Now you have the burden. What will be the result? You will naturally marry the girl. And then? Then there comes every year a crying brat until there are four or five. At the fifth the poor creature dies and Aunt Ursul can then take the young brood and raise them. But I tell you, that won't do, by any means! I would not undertake it should you offer me a ton of gold for each child."

Aunt Ursul had spoken so excitedly and in so loud a voice that Lambert was glad when, turning, he saw Catherine following slowly at a great distance, her head bowed down and she often plucking a wood-flower.

"How can you talk in that way, aunt?" said Lambert.

"To you it would indeed be pleasanter should I utter what first comes into the mouth, and say yea, and amen, to what you dumbheads have hatched out. Furthermore, I have no sympathy for you, sir. You have prepared your own soup. You must eat it yourself. Poor girl! Thrust out into the world naked and bare, so to speak, and with such eyes—just like your sainted mother's—by which all men were captivated. This is itself already a heaven-appearing misfortune. I can sing a song about it. Why do you laugh, you green woodpecker? Do you think, since now, in my fifty-seventh year, I am not as slim as an osier-switch and as smooth as an eel, I could not turn the heads of the men at seventeen? You are getting on beautifully. I tell you how foolish they were, though it isn't worth while to say it, for they are all so. But I had half a dozen on every finger, and your girl has as yet but two."

"Surely I do not understand you, aunt," said Lambert, whose anxiety kept increasing as long as she kept talking in her peculiar way.

"Well, then, I will speak plainly," said Ursul, after she had cast a rapid glance toward Catherine. "This morning—I was just raking up my hay—your brother came with such a leap over the gate that my first impulse was to give him one over the head, and, distracted and wild, to my horror, began to speak so incoherently, that no one besides me, who know him from childhood, could have gathered his meaning; saying that he must shoot himself dead since you could not both marry her, and other foolish talk, all showing that he is madly and blindly in love with the girl."

Lambert was frightened, as he now heard from the mouth of Aunt Ursul what Catherine herself had told him a few minutes before. So the bad temper had not been blown away by the first morning wind that fanned the cheeks of the hunter, as he had hoped it would be. He had carried it at least as far as Aunt Ursul's.

"Surely you have set his head right, aunt?" said Lambert.

"First set right the head of that pine," said Aunt Ursul, pointing to an immense tree which had been shattered by lightning so that its top now held by the bark, hung to the trunk. "And then, sir, you did not do right in not keeping your promise to bring the young man a wife as you have done for yourself."

"I promised nothing of the kind," replied Lambert earnestly. "It was impossible for me to believe that Conrad was serious when he called after me, as I was already trotting off down the valley: 'Bring back with you a wife for each of us!' I never thought of it again—especially not when heaven threw in my way a poor orphan, and I offered her, forsaken by the whole world, a refuge with me. You see, aunt, that I am indeed blameless."

"Then give him the girl," said Ursul.

"Sooner my life," earnestly replied Lambert.

"I would like to know," said Ursul, "whether I cannot justly say that beauty is a woman's misfortune, and I suppose you will admit it. Nor is it less so for the men who are bewitched by it. What do the poor creatures gain by it? Nothing more than the turtledoves which I found covered with blood near your house. What do you gain by it? Just as much as the two eagles who, on account of those doves, tore the flesh from each other's bodies. Alas, poor women! unhappy women!"

"Conrad will listen to reason," said Lambert, with trembling lips.

"I do not know," replied Ursul, shaking her large head. "It often happens that men-folks become reasonable, but they usually wait until it is too late. So I fear it will also be this time. Now he has gone into the woods, and heaven knows how long he will wander about there, and that at a time when we cannot spare a single man—and him least of all."

"He won't fail us when we need him," said Lambert.

"He failed us last year, and did we not need him then? But so men are, and especially you young men. You make a hunting match, or get up a race, or, at a wedding, dance the soles off your feet, and do everything as it pleases you, and the rest you let go as it pleases God. We saw it last year. How I talked, and preached, urging you to watchfulness, after I saw that General Abercrombie in Albany did not bestir himself, and naturally your hands were lying in your laps. I preached to deaf ears. Afterward when the abominable French broke in and sunk, and burned, and murdered after their wicked heart's desire—yes, now every one protected his own head as best he could. But how many houses might still stand, how many wives and children could to-day yet look at the lovely sun and praise their heavenly Father, if you from the first had stood together as it became intelligent men? And now, Lambert, there stands my horse and I do not know what more to say to you; so help yourself out of the mire

and me on my horse; and, as to what concerns the
lady, I will come again to-morrow, or you can bring
her to me.   I will not bite her.   Have no care.   To-
day I won't stay longer.   God protect you, Lambert.
Give my compliments to the lady.   What is her
name?"

"Catherine Weise," said Lambert.   "She is an
orphan.   Her father, who was a preacher, and, out
of love for his people, emigrated with them, she lost
eight days before the ship reached New York."

"Catherine," said Ursul.   "Our dear Father in
heaven!   So I always wanted to call my daughter,
should I have one.   Both my sainted grandmothers
had that name.   Nay, things happen alike.   Compliments to the girl, who seems to be a well-behaved
person, and God protect you, Lambert."

The Amazon arranged her clothes, which was somewhat difficult, as she sat like a man in the saddle,
chirruped to her horse, gave him a hard cut over the
neck, and trotted briskly away from the edge of the
woods where they had stood, down the hill, over the
meadow, until she reached the road which led from
the creek to the other farm-houses.

The young man looked at the retreating figure with
sad glances and a deep sigh.   He heard behind him a
light step.   He turned eagerly and opened his arms
to the beloved one.   But Catherine shook her handsome head.   Her large, inquiring dark eyes, in which
there were still some traces of tears, rested on his
face.

"For God's sake!" exclaimed Lambert, "why do you look in such a strange way, Catherine? What have we to do with others? I love you."

"And I you," said Catherine, "but it must happen."

"What must happen? Catherine, dear Catherine," cried Lambert.

"Come," said the maiden, "let us sit down here and talk with each other quietly, very quietly."

She sat down on the trunk of a half-buried pine and looked thoughtfully before her.

Lambert seated himself at her side. He wished to speak, but before he could find the right word, Catherine raised her eyes and said:

"See, Lambert, how much you have kindly done for me, a poor girl, and I could not do otherwise than give you back the only thing I have—my all—and love you with all the strength of my soul, with every drop of blood in my heart. I could not do otherwise, and it will be so as long as I live, and after this life throughout eternity. But, Lambert, it was not right for me that, in addition to the much and the beautiful that you have given me, I should also take your love. I felt this from the first day on, and I tried to prevent your seeing my love, though I confess it was a hard task."

Catherine's voice trembled, but she held back the tears that were ready to break from her eyes, and continued:

"I felt from the beginning—and I have said to my-

self, and promised thousands of times—that I would
be a maid-servant to you and your parents and relatives, and, should you bring home a wife, I would also
serve her and her children, and so help, as much as
I could, to promote your happiness and that of all
related to you.   When I yesterday learned that you
no longer have parents I fled.   I wished to flee,
while a voice, which I only now rightly understand,
said that it would come about as it now has come,
and as it should not have come.   I have not listened
to the voice of my conscience, and the punishment
follows at its heels.   Your brother is angry at you on
my account.   Your aunt has left you in anger on my
account.   What a bàd girl I must be, could I calmly
look on and see how unhappy I am making him for
whom I would give my blood, drop by drop.   For
this reason it must take place.   You have given me
permission to go where I will—and God will guide
my steps."

Having uttered these words she arose, pale, having
her hands folded under her bosom, and her tearless
eyes having a far-off look.

Immediately Lambert stood up before her, and her
eyes met his, which shone with a wonderfully clear
and steady light.   "Catherine!"

More he did not say.   But it was the right word
and the right tone—a cordial tone full of tender suggestion, and yet so firm, so true, that it resounded
again in the heart of the maiden: "Catherine!"

and filled her soul with sweet pleasure. What she
had just said, in the bitter feeling of her injured pride,
and in her painful conviction that she must subordi-
nate her own happiness and the happiness of him she
loved—it now seemed to her but idle breath, like the
wind sweeping above through the rustling tops of the
pines and below over the bending grass of the meadow. The pines stood firm, the grass rose again, and
everything remained as it was before—yes, more beautiful and delightful than before. What was now her
pride except a small additional offering that she
brought to her beloved who would not be happy without her—who without her could not be happy? This
Lambert said to her again and again; and she said to
him that separation from her beloved and death would
be the same for her, and that she would never again
think of it, but that she could live for him and be
happy with him.

So they sat a long time at the edge of the primitive forest in the shadow of the venerable trees—before them the sunlit prairie with its bending flowers
and grass, alone—speaking in whispers, as though
the mottled butterflies which were moving about the
flowers must not hear. And if a bird happened to fly
past uttering his warning cry, frightened, they crowded
close to each other and then laughed, happy that
they were alone and might sink into each other's
arms and say what they had already said a hundred
times, and yet did not get tired of saying and hearing
it.

Then they formed plans for the future—far-reaching plans—that during the fall they would clear at least yet five acres, and that they would in any case keep the calf of which Aunt Ursul had the care, and whether it would not be best to partition off a chamber in the upper story of the house, leaving sufficient space for the store-room; and, as the stairway was very narrow and steep, they would make a new one. They must also not fail to have a suitable garden in which to raise greens and gooseberries and currants; and a honeysuckle-arbor, such as Catherine had in her father's garden, there surely must be, though Lambert was not sure that he quite understood what Catherine meant by a honeysuckle-arbor.

The ascending sun suggested their return home. Lambert was disinclined to leave the woods in whose shade the complete fullness of his happiness had been revealed. But Catherine said: "No, you must not on my account neglect a single duty that rests on you. Otherwise your friends, who consider it a misfortune that you have taken up a poor girl like me, will be right. So you must yet to-day ride to your neighbors with your compliments. They would take it amiss should you not do it, and they would be right. It is your duty to inform them about your journey, which you undertook for their best interest as well as your own. They will be pleased to see you again, and that everything has turned out so well."

"And where shall I leave you, in the meantime?"

asked Lambert, as they now walked slowly along the creek toward the house.

"Where a woman should be—at home," said Catherine.

"I unwillingly leave you there," said Lambert. "I do not believe I could return before evening, however I might hasten. It is six miles to Adam Bellinger's, who lives near the mouth of the creek and who is the last of us six who prepared the petition to the governor. On the way I must stop three times, or rather four times, for I must not ride past my old Uncle Ditmar. It is impossible for me to leave you so long alone, since the French are stirring again, and I do not know how far they have come already."

"Here good advice is dear," said Catherine laughing mischievously. "You can't take me along to-day, after you yesterday went far out of your way so that your neighbors should not see what a wonderful rarity you had brought with you on your return from your journey."

"Nor shall it be different," said Lambert, but little pained by the gentle raillery, accompanied as it was with a kiss. "Though you do not go the whole distance, you can at least go as far as Ditmar's."

Catherine arched her eyebrows: "Are you quite sure that I should be kindly received there?" she asked gently.

"Quite sure," said Lambert, earnestly, "the more so as my aunt was unfriendly to you before. As far as I know her she has no stronger wish than to repair the mischief.   Believe me, Catherine, a better heart than Aunt Ursul's cannot be found, though the severe fate that has befallen her has made her peculiar and unmannerly."

"Tell me about it," said Catherine.

"It is a dreadful history," said Lambert, "and I would rather not rehearse it; but you will think otherwise of my aunt when you meet her, and so let it be.

"It is now thirteen years—it was in 'forty-four and I was nineteen—when war broke out between the English and the French, which they call King George's war.   Neither the English nor the French could raise many men, so they had to rely on the Indians, each party trying by every means to win them to itself and set them against the opposite party.   Now, the English had a treaty of a long standing with the Six Nations; but at this time they also began to waver and to unite with the French, who knew better how to flatter them.   So many fell away, and entered into secret or open partnership with our foes.   The uncertainty daily increased.   Nobody had any assurance of his life.   The Germans here on the Mohawk, and especially on the creek, had hitherto escaped; but the danger came nearer and nearer to us, and then it was that we went to our work with a rifle on the shoulder, and when father, with the help of a couple of blacks from Virginia—secured for the occasion—strengthened the block-house as it is now.   Before, it was more open.

"Nicolas Herkimer settled on the Mohawk, and several others followed his example. Most of them, however, took the matter more lightly, and said the French or Indians should only come on; they would soon show them the road, and send them home with bloody heads. About this they debated with Uncle Ditmar, and became angry at him since he was always full of courage and of bitter hatred of the French whom he had already learned to know on the other side, where they had burned his parents' house and driven them from their home. He thought that should we wait until the French came to us it would be altogether too late. It was a shame that now everybody should think only of himself. All should assemble here, and on the Mohawk, and on the Schoharie; that no one should stay at home who could fire off a rifle, and that some should go to meet the French, and pay them back, in their own territory, what before and since they have done to us. Perhaps the old man was right, but nobody listened to him. Then came the year 'forty-six, when the French with their Indians swept through the valley of the Mohawk as far as Schenectady and Albany, and destroyed and robbed what they found, and killed and scalped what came in their way, and committed every conceivable horror. My uncle could stand it no longer. He went out with his four sons—my cousins —of whom the eldest was twenty-six and the youngest nineteen. Aunt Ursul would not stay at home,

but went along, with her rifle on her shoulder, just
as you saw her awhile ago, and they carried on war
by themselves and killed many French and Indians,
until they were resting on a certain day among a
small clump of trees on the open prairie and, not noticing, were overrun from all sides. There my aunt
saw her sons fall, one after the other, while she was
loading the guns. At last old Ditmar was struck by
a stray bullet and sank at her feet apparently dead.
Aunt Ursul fired off the gun she had loaded once
more and laid a Frenchman low, seized it by the muz-
zle, and swinging the butt on high she rushed out and
struck about her so, that the Indians themselves,
at sight of such bravery, did not kill her, but over-
powered her, and tied her, and took her along as
prisoner. They likewise took uncle, who gave signs
of life, when an Indian had already torn his scalp half
off. Perhaps they intended to spare them for a later,
more painful death. But it did not go as far as that,
thank God! for the troop which was taking them
along was attacked by another tribe, which held with
the English, and they were killed to the last man.
So my aunt, after a couple of months, came again,
robbed of her stalwart sons, with her husband, whose
mind has never since been quite right, and who has
lived on for months and years without uttering a word,
though attending to his work like anyone else."

Lambert ceased speaking. Catherine took his
hand and, with gentle pressure, held it.

So they went, hand in hand, along the creek. Here and there a pair of summer-ducks came out of the reeds and flew, swift as an arrow, toward the woods. Fish sprang up in the crystal-clear water. The rushes waved. The flowers and grass on the prairie swayed in the tepid wind. The sun poured down its golden rays. But it seemed to both as if there had fallen a veil over the clear, spring morning.

"I wish I had not told you this—at least not to-day," said Lambert.

"And I thank you that you did so," said Catherine. "The happiness would be too great were our good fortune without a shadow. Did you not find me help-less, forsaken, poor as a beggar, pressed to the ground by care and grief, and did you not, without a mo-ment's hesitation, stretch out your hand to pick me out of the dust? So I will hold it fast—your dear hand—and help you carry the cares and burdens of life, and with you go into the battle, if it must be, as good Aunt Ditmar did, whom may God bless for her bravery, and whose pardon I heartily beg for the in-jury I did her in my feelings. Now I can see why she who has suffered so dreadfully cannot, like other good people, heartily rejoice over the good fortune which comes to them before her eyes. Poor soul! She no longer believes in good fortune."

"Perhaps it is also something else," said Lambert thoughtfully, and after a short pause proceeded: "See, Catherine, I love you so dearly, and have

kept still so long, that I would like to tell you about
everything that passes through my mind. So I will
also tell you this: I do not know, but I believe that
my aunt would be better pleased were Conrad in my
place. She has not forgotten that she carried the
youngster, when a small and helpless creature, in her
arms, and has always loved him as though she were
his own mother. So Conrad has also hung to her;
and, on account of the Ditmars, the difficulty arose
between him and our father. Conrad wanted to go
and live at Ditmar's, and father forbid it to the eleven-
year-old youngster. The very Indian tribe to which
Conrad fled had rescued the Ditmars. I believe he
was himself present, though I do not know, since he
has never said a word about it; nor has aunt, to
whom he may have forbidden it. All this aunt has
never forgotten."

"And shall not forget it," observed Catherine with
animation. "See, Lambert, now that we have honorably acknowledged that we love one another, I am
no longer so timid. We must now be equally honest
toward the others. Your aunt knows it, you say,
and she will adapt herself to the actual state of
affairs. Conrad must also know it, and then he won't
be angry at you any longer. It perhaps sounds a little bold, but if I am indeed pleasing to him, let me
manage it, Lambert. I will tame the young bear for
you."

Lambert shook his head, and had again to laugh as

he now looked into the face of the beloved one, which beamed with happiness as before. "Yes, yes, who could withstand you? Who would not willingly do what you wish?"

They had reached the block-house, and entered the open door. Lambert looked about the room with as much wonder as though he now saw it for the first time. About the hearth, on the shelves, there hung and stood kettles, pitchers and pots clean and burnished. They had heretofore always been in confusion. On the hearth itself the live coals glimmered under the ashes, and only needed to be uncovered and fanned again to start the fire. Near by lay the fire-wood carefully piled up. The table was brightly scoured. The chairs were set in order. The floor was sprinkled with white sand. The hunting and fishing apparatus neatly hung against the wall. The small mirror which, dusty and dull, had hitherto leaned in a dark corner, had found a suitable place between the silhouettes of his parents, while they were encircled with simple garlands.

"You best one!" said Lambert, as with deep emotion he locked the beloved one in his arms. "You will prove the good angel of us all."

"To that may God help me!" ejaculated Catherine. "And now, Lambert, we must think about the obligations resting on us. While you go and feed Hans, I will prepare our noonday meal. After dinner we will start, for I suppose you mean to take me

along. Now, no more talking; we have already
trifled away too much time."

She drove out the beloved one with kisses and
scolding, and then turned to her work, which she
pushed forward in a lively manner, though she often
pressed her hand on her heart, which it seemed would
burst with sheer happiness. Wherever she looked,
she, in imagination, saw the form of her beloved—the
true, good, thoughtful eyes; the face embrowned by
exposure, with its handsome, clear expression; the
powerful frame, which moved with such calm assurance. In the crackling of the fire; in the measured
tick-tack of the old Swartzwald clock, she seemed
ever to hear his deep, friendly voice; and she mentally
recalled the words he had said to her, and trembled
with pleasure as she thought how her name rang out
from his lips: "Catherine!" So she had always
been called. Her father, friends, neighbors, all the
world had called her Catherine, and yet it seemed
as though to-day she had heard it for the first time.

Oh! everything had turned out so different and so
much better than she had dared to hope. How
doubtingly she had looked toward the land with fixed
eyes, which had already learned to weep on the tort-
ure-ship. What more could it bring her besides terrible, inconceivable misery? How unhappy she had
yesterday felt on her arrival, and again this morning.
Could she then now be in reality happy, so very happy
that her dear, dead father, were he still living, could

wish for her nothing better—nothing more desirable?

Catherine bowed her head and folded her hands in prayer, and then looked up with brightened glances.

"Yes," said she softly, "he would have blessed our engagement with his fatherly, priestly blessing. I can call myself his before men, as I am before God and in my own heart. And though I have no friend, male or female, to rejoice with us and to wish us joy, I am on that account none the less his and he mine. But I will make friends of the whole world—the strange old aunt and the wild Conrad. I am no longer afraid of anybody—of anything."

So spoke Catherine to herself as she was setting the table, and yet she was badly scared as, at that moment, she heard the stamping of a horse before the house, and a loud human voice calling:

"He, holla! Lambert Sternberg!"

Trembling, she laid down the plates and stepped to the door to see the caller, who again and again screamed: "Lambert Sternberg! He, holla, Lambert Sternberg!"

CHAPTER VII

Before the house, on a long-limbed, lean horse, whose panting flanks and hanging head showed that he had just completed a long and rapid trip, a young man had stopped. On Catherine's appearance he forgot to shut the large mouth which he had opened in calling. His long, flaxen hair hung down in strands from under his large, three-cornered hat upon his narrow shoulders. The sweat poured from his freckled, saturated, long face, and his dull, water-blue eyes had a frightened look as Catherine, aghast, called out:

"For God's sake, what has happened?"

"Where is he?" stammered he on the horse, and turned his eyes in every direction.

"You are looking for Lambert Sternberg?" asked Catherine.

The rider bowed.

"I will call him. Dismount and rest yourself a moment. I will soon be back," said Catherine.

The rider did as the young girl had told him, climbed in a tired way out of the high saddle, and tied his horse to the iron ring. As Catherine turned to go, Lambert came around the house. He was leading Hans by the halter, and called out:

"God bless you, Adam Bellinger! What brings you here?"

"The French are here!" replied Adam.

Lambert started, and looked quickly toward Catherine, who on her part kept her large, questioning eyes fixed on him.

"What does that mean?" asked Lambert. "Where are they? What do you know, Adam? By the thousand, man, speak!"

"I know nothing," said Adam. "My father sent me."

"What for? What is to be done?"

"I was in the field," said Adam, "when my father came running up, saying that I must unharness and saddle the mare; that Herkimer had been there; that the French were on the march; and that I should report it everywhere, and that this afternoon all should come to his house to consult as to what was to be done."

"Then it cannot be so very bad," said Lambert, breathing more freely. "Herkimer is a man of sense, and would not ask us to come to his house if there was very pressing danger to our own homes. But how did you learn that I had returned?"

"I was at Aunt Ursul's, who sent me here to tell you that she was going to the meeting, and that if you should not wish to leave the young lady, who may indeed be your bride, alone, you should take her along and leave her at Eisenlord's on the way, or at

Voltz', where the women intend to remain at home, or at our house."

"It is well," said Lambert, as he took the hand of Catherine, standing by him still and pale. "Now come in, Adam Bellinger, and take a bite and a drink. You appear to need it, and the poor beast too. We will be ready in ten minutes."

Lambert shoved up the movable crib, while Catherine went into the house and brought out a loaf of bread which Adam cut in pieces for his horse. Then they all went in and sat down to the hastily prepared meal, to which Adam addressed himself so earnestly that he had little time to answer Lambert's many questions.

Catherine learned enough, as she silently listened, to form a conception of the real situation. She had often heard Lambert speak of Nicolas Herkimer, one of the richest and noblest German settlers, who owned a large farm and a castle-like house on the Mohawk, at the mouth of Canada Creek. The year before, during Belletre's raid, he had been of great service to the settlements. The governor had given him a captain's commission, and had intrusted him, for the future, with the defense of the neighboring German districts.

"He will already have formed his plans," said Lambert. "We on the creek will doubtless have to look out for ourselves, we are pushed ahead so far. There shall be nothing lacking with us, though I did not expect to have the murdering incendiaries here so soon again."

Out of Lambert's entire being spoke the settled courage of a man who well knew the threatened danger, but was resolved to defy it, come what would. His eyes sought Catherine's, who went quietly back and forth serving the men, and whose large, glistening eyes said: "You see, beloved, I am, like you, quiet and self-contained."

Adam seemed to have forgotten all his fear, while engaged in eating and drinking. He looked up at Catherine, when she filled his plate for the second time, bowing with a friendly grin. At last he slowly laid down his knife and fork and looked about him contentedly, as though he would say: "One sits here a good deal more comfortably than in the cursed high saddle of the mare, who threw me at every step from one side to the other."

"Are you ready, Adam?" asked Lambert, who had risen and had hung about him his rifle.

"Indeed," replied Adam, "but hardly the mare. The poor beast is not accustomed to anything like this."

"I will water her, and saddle Hans," said Lambert.

Catherine followed him to the door. Lambert caught her hand and said: "Catherine, I thank you, I thank you with my whole heart. I now know that I need cast no more reproaches on myself."

"You should not have cast any," said Catherine.

"Your affairs are mine   Your fate is mine. I live and die with you."

"And so will I give every drop of my blood for you," said Lambert, "but I hope to God that there are yet many good days appointed us. It cannot for the present have much significance. Conrad, who was up there for a week, and in the region from which they must come, surely knows more about our enemies than anyone else; and he told me that there is at least no immediate danger."

"So I think, too," said Catherine, "and for that reason I will ask a favor of you, Lambert. You have on my account slightly neglected your duty. Had you returned alone you would yesterday already have seen and spoken with your friends, for you would have taken the road through the valley instead of through the woods. To-day it is fortunate that your friend Adam has found us, for you might easily have failed to be where you belong. This is not right, and lies heavy on my mind. Now you have a long ride. I know well that Hans can carry us both, but he will go better if you alone ride him. And then what would be the result should everyone, on such an occasion, drag his wife with him? The others also stay at home. You will leave me here, Lambert. Is it not so?"

"Now it is getting to be time," said Adam Bellinger, coming out of the door.

Lambert stood irresolute. He saw no danger in

leaving Catherine alone, but it was very trying for him to separate himself from her just at this time.

"Conrad may come back to his dinner and find the house deserted. Surely it is better, Lambert, that I stay here."

"Well, as you will," said Lambert.

He again unbuckled the pillion that he had put upon Hans.

"Does not the maiden go along?" asked Adam, who was already mounted.

Lambert did not answer.

"Well then, good-bye, young lady; and best thanks. Hot! Mare!"

He turned his horse, which left the crib unwillingly. Catherine flew into Lambert's arms.

"May you live happy, beloved. I hope you are not displeased with me?"

"With you?"

His lips trembled. Silently he pressed Catherine to his breast; then with a mighty effort he tore himself away, swung himself upon Hans, galloped after his companion, who was trotting ahead on his long-limbed horse, and at every step of the animal flew up in the air, while his sharp elbows moved up and down like wings.

CHAPTER VIII

Lambert soon overtook the awkward rider. The two young men trotted on for a time side by side without speaking, until suddenly the mare, panting, stood still. Adam, having thus been thrown upon the neck of the beast, remarked that the mare was a very intelligent creature, and well knew that it was impossible for her to keep going at such a gait; that in such a case she always stopped to give the rider time for reflection; and that he had always found that one also finally reaches his destination by going on a walk, and that far easier.

"But also so much later," said Lambert, impatiently. "If you are absolutely unable to keep up with me I must leave you and ride on ahead."

"For God's sake!" cried Adam, and thrust his heels so forcibly into the sides of the mare that she sprang forward, and again fell into a trot. "For God's sake! that will soon fail."

"You are a coward," said Lambert, "in that you are put to the blush by a girl."

He turned back in the saddle toward the block-house before it should disappear from his sight behind the forest-encompassed, rocky hill around which they were winding. Catherine had not left her place in front of the door. Though uncertain whether she could see the salutation he waved his hand to her, and then the rocks hid her from his sight.

An indescribable sadness fell upon Lambert and it did not lack much but he would have turned Hans about and gone back at full speed. But with a strong determination he overcame his painful emotion. "I am just as great a coward," said he to himself, "and even a greater one, for I know better about what is going on, and nothing that I do for her should be burdensome to me."

"You may well talk," Adam broke in upon Lambert's self-communings.

"Why?" asked Lambert.

"Should they pull the scalp from over your ears no rooster would crow after that; but my mother would weep her eyes out."

"Perhaps there may be somebody who would rather see my scalp on my head than on an Indian's girdle."

"Do you mean the young lady?" asked Adam, opening his mouth from ear to ear, and for a moment letting go of the horn of the saddle, and pointing back over his shoulder with his thumb.

"Perhaps," said Lambert.

"Don't trouble yourself about that," said Adam, in a comforting tone. "Then I will marry her. It is already a long time since mother wanted me to marry. But you know I would not take just anybody. The girl pleases me."

"So!" said Lambert.

"Yes," said Adam. "Barbara and Gussie and Annie would doubtless at first cry a little, but that would come right in time. I believe that Fritz and August Volz are already engaged to Barbara and Gussie, and we have always thought that you would marry Annie."

"With or without a scalp?" asked Lambert.

Adam thought this such a capital joke that he stopped the mare to press his fists into his sides and break out in ringing laughter. A fish-hawk, which had plunged into the creek among the reeds, flew away frightened, while his warning voice rang out.

"My God!" said Adam, "I really thought it was already one of the mean French, or red-skins."

"Have you during this time of terror heard of them?" asked Lambert as they were riding along.

"Once," said Adam, "about a month ago. Father went to Schenectady with the wheat, and I was alone in the field, when little Anton came running and cried out: 'The Indians have swum across the creek and are at our house.' Fear so flew into my legs that I did not know where my head stood, and I wanted to go right home to help the women. But when I again got my breath I was standing before Eisenlord's door. The old man was at home, and at once sent his youngest son to Peter Volz', whence soon there came the old man himself and Fritz and August. Then we went courageously forward, though the crying women did not want us to go. On the way Christian Eisenlord and young Peter Volz joined us, so that we were six or seven, although apparently there could not much reliance be placed on me, since I almost cried my eyes out from pity and heartache that I should now find our house burned down, and my beautiful Bless and the four English hogs, that I had just that morning bought of John Mertens, driven away, and mother and Barbara and Gussie and Annie scalped. But as we came out of the woods, through which we had carefully skulked, there stood our house undisturbed; and the women were standing before the door scolding little Anton, who was crying bitterly."

"How about the Indians?" asked Lambert.

"You must not interrupt me, if I am to tell my story in an orderly way," said Adam. "Where was I?"

"At Anton, who was crying bitterly."

"The poor boy!" said Adam. "I could not blame him. He should have gone in and covered the Indian—who was about naked, so that the women were ashamed."

"Then there really was one there?"

"Yes, indeed; and he had swum through the creek, and lay on the hearth as drunk as a red-skin can be, and snored so that we could hear him outdoors. Then the others had a good laugh at my expense, and, since, they have constantly jeered me about the

drunken fellow, though one should not paint the devil
on the wall. I indeed could do nothing about it.
But little Anton should have been wiser. On account of what took place then, they would not believe
my message to-day; and had I not said and sworn
that Herkimer himself had told my father, they would
have remained at home, except Aunt Ursul, who immediately saddled both her horses."

"So! Has uncle also gone along?" asked Lambert.

"We shall soon know," said Adam. "I will call."
They stopped before the Ditmar house. Adam rose
in his stirrups, put both hands to his mouth and
screamed so loud that the doves on the roof were
frightened, and Melac, the watch-dog, in the yard, .
began to bark and howl fearfully. "He, holla!
Christian Ditmar! holla, he!" However the long
figure of old Ditmar did not appear at the upper-half
of the door, through which one could see the interior.

Lambert thought best to go right on and not call
at William Teichert's. His farm lay somewhat to
one side, at the edge of the woods which here bore
back from the creek in a great bend and came back
to it again near Peter Volz' yard. Here indeed they
had to stop, for mother Volz had seen the riders
from a distance, and stood before the door with a
pitcher of home-brewed beer in each hand, which
Peter, her youngest son, had just drawn fresh from
the barrel. Mother Volz was much excited, and

great tears rolled over her big cheeks as she handed the pitchers to the riders, at the same time scolding the French and her Peter, who would go to the meeting and leave her—an old, helpless woman—alone, the good-for-nothing!

"If I am good for nothing," said Peter, "I cannot help you, mother. But I must always stay at home and play the baby; that is just as it is."

"Yes, that is the case," said Adam, smacking his lips forcibly over his beer, "and the rest of us must have a hard time of it."

"Then give me the mare and you stay here," said the courageous Peter.

Adam was not disinclined to accept so agreeable an offer, and began to climb out of the saddle when the mare, perhaps misunderstanding the motion of the rider, or because she perceived that she was near her own stable, suddenly started on a trot, to Adam's disappointment and Lambert's satisfaction, whose impatience at the unnecessary loitering had become very great.

Now, however, thanks to the mare's fixed purpose to end her unusual labor for the day, without stopping, she went on faster and faster—so that Adam held convulsively to the horn of the saddle, while his long, yellow hair flew about his ears—on along the creek, past John Eisenlord's house, where the women hastened to the door, and called, and wondering looked after those who were rushing past. Thus they went faster and faster until the mare stopped in Bellinger's yard with a jerk and threw her rider over her head in the sand at the feet of his mother and three sisters and younger brother. His mother called out:

"Run, little Anton! and open the stable for the mare, so that she does not crush her skull against the door—the poor beast!"

No one felt concerned for Adam. In fact, this was the usual way in which the mare, after such a trip, returned her rider. He soon got up and rubbed his long legs groaning, while the women surrounded Lambert and inquired about his journey; when he got back; and why in the world he yesterday took the rough road through the woods? how his maid-servant behaved? and why he had brought one from a distance of fifty miles, when he could easily have found one—and perhaps a better one—near by?

Lambert briefly thanked them for their kind inquiries, ascertained how long since the men had gone, spurred his horse and, with a brief salutation, trotted away, thus filling the beautiful blonde Annie with not a little anxiety, and compelling her to listen to the remarks of her sisters, Barbara and Gussie:

"Now one can clearly see, what we always thought, that Lambert Sternberg did not take that long journey to New York on account of the pines."

Annie replied that she cared nothing for Lambert, and that Fritz and August Volz had also not yet declared themselves. The mother took Annie's part, and the dispute threatened to become serious, when it happily occurred to them that they had not once asked Adam what sort of a person the new girl was.

They now learned from the keen rider, who had gone into the house and was rubbing his shins with brandy, that, in no case was Lambert to have her, but that he himself was to marry the girl as soon as the Indians had taken Lambert's scalp, and that he and Lambert had come to a complete agreement on that matter.

While Catherine's fate was thus discussed in the Bellinger family, Lambert pushed along on a fast trot to regain lost time. He had gathered from the questions of the women, and still more from the tone in which they were put, that the way in which he had dealt was not thought favorably of. He was yesterday persuaded of this, and to escape this neighborhood interference he had taken the road through the woods. He felt grieved and angry at his aunt, who alone could have spread abroad the knowledge of his return and his relation to Catherine. Still he said to himself that, since all must shortly know it, it was best they should know it as soon as possible. He saw how difficult his position in the community would be—as indeed it should be—so long as Catherine was not his wife; possibly even after that; that, at all events, it was his duty to make his relation to Catherine clear to all eyes. He determined yet to-day,

should opportunity offer, to speak to the minister and
to seek the advice and help of that excellent man.

He had now come out of what was properly the
valley of the creek, near its mouth. Toward the
right of him lay the broad German Flats, in the fork
between the creek and the Mohawk. The land, long
rescued from the primitive forest, was rich, and there
were unbroken lines of successive settlements, with
a small church and a parsonage in the midst on a hill.
Before him, on the other side of the Mohawk, whose
clear waters glanced between its bushy shores, there
stood out also on a hill, what looked like a small for-
tification. This, the purposed end of his journey,
was Nicolas Herkimer's stately house.

He now discovered that, as he had feared, he
would not be the last one to arrive. In the even
reaches between corn-fields and bushes those coming
on foot or on horseback singly, or by twos, or threes,
from different directions, could be seen, all moving
toward one point. There was a house conveniently
situated on this side of the river, diagonally across
from Herkimer's farm, where Hans Haberkorn, the
ferryman, lived.

Here, a few minutes afterward, Lambert met the
men whom he had from a distance seen coming. By
them he was greeted very cordially, as though all had
heard of his journey to New York, but not of his return. They wanted to know how the matters had re-
sulted and especially what he had heard in the city

about the war in Europe; whether the French had really, the year before at Roszbach, been so helplessly slaughtered, and whether the king of Prussia was this year going to take the field against his countless enemies.

Lambert told them what he knew, and on his part sought information about things at home. Of the five or six men who thus happened to meet, each gave his impressions as best he could, from which it appeared that there were nearly as many different opinions as there were men, in the small gathering. Yes, while they were eagerly attacking Hans Haberkorn's rum, they became so warm that they seemed to have forgotten why they were there, until Lambert's urgency induced them to go on.

Hans Haberkorn thought there was no hurry and that they could just as well consult here as at Herkimer's. The rest, however, would not stay behind. They tied their horses in a row, under an open shed, to the manger, and went upon the river; and on the short passage across renewed their debate with increased earnestness, so that it did not lack much of going from words to blows on the small scow.

On this account it was fortunate that, as they landed on the other side, others joined them, of whom some had crossed before, while others, coming from the other side, awaited the landing of the ferry-boat so that they could go on together. Over the greeting they for the moment forgot their contention, but they had proceeded but a few steps before the war of words began again as before, while those who came up afterward mingled in the crowd and took part on one or the other side. So, scolding and quarreling, they reached the front yard of Herkimer's house.

CHAPTER IX

There might have been a hundred who were here assembled, all German settlers from the Mohawk, from the creek, and some even from Schoharie, for that far had the circumspect Herkimer sent his message. In the tall, often giant-like men, who sat in long rows on the benches under the projecting roof of the house, in the shade, or moved about on the open, sunny lawn, nobody would have recognized the descendants of the pale and emaciated immigrants who, in their time, landed in the harbor of New York and of Philadelphia from pest-ships, in an inhospitable country. So thought Lambert, as he cast his eye over the assembly and looked at those nearer, whom he knew and soon singled out. There was first the distinguished form of Nicolas Herkimer himself, with broad shoulders, on which the long, grayish hair fell, and the clear, blue eyes, which to-day appeared brighter and more thoughtful than usual as he spoke with one and another, and then again looked at the position of the sun to see whether the hour appointed for the meeting had come. There was the minister Rosenkrantz, with his kind, friendly face as storm-tried and weather-browned as that of any of his people, from whom he was distinguished only by his black

clothes and his large snuff-box, which he was constantly turning about in his fingers. There were his
neighbors, the Volzes, and the Eisenlords, father
and sons, and William Teichert, and old Adam Bellinger; and at last he also discovered, at the farthest
corner, his uncle, Christian Ditmar, still as ever and
brooding with his fur cap drawn far down over his
face. Lambert was trying to press through to the
old man, as Richard, Herkimer's youngest son, of
the same age as Conrad, and a dear friend of both
brothers, touched his shoulder.

"God bless you, Lambert! You have come back at
the right time, I should say. Where is your brother?"

Lambert informed him that this morning Conrad
went hunting, and had not yet returned when he himself left home.

"This will be very unpleasant news for father," said
Richard. "He has already asked a couple of times
for both of you. There he comes himself. I will
afterward talk with you, Lambert."

It was painful enough for Lambert that he was
obliged to give the same information to the honored
man who so heartily welcomed him. "I knew it already from your aunt," said Herkimer, "but I hoped
that he had meanwhile come. It is very unpleasant
that he fails us. I hear that he has been for eight
days at the lake, and surely knows more about the
movements of our enemies than any one of us. To
be sure I have on the whole been well informed, but

it would be desirable to have some one on whom I could call. What did he tell you?"

"Only this," replied Lambert, and then told Herkimer the little he had learned from Conrad; that the Onondaga Indians were assembled in large number, and that it was Conrad's impression that it was not for a good purpose.

"That agrees altogether with my other reports," said Nicolas Herkimer. "These rascals have already for a long time played false, and we shall doubtless soon have them on our necks. Listen, Lambert; I have thought of placing you in an important position, and before we enter upon our consultation I wish to come to an understanding with you. Mr. Rosenkrantz, a moment."

The preacher drew near and heartily greeted Lambert, and began at once to ask about his journey, but Herkimer quickly interrupted the talkative minister.

"That will do as well later, dominie," said he, "we have now something more important to think of. I wish to explain our plan to Lambert, on whom we can rely in any event. This, Lambert, is our plan: After our losses of last year we are, in any case, too weak for open warfare against an enemy far exceeding us in number and able to choose his own time and place for attack. The only thing left for us to do is, by constant and regular scouting, as well as possible to learn his movements, so that, before an actual attack follows, we can retire to our fortified points.

One of these naturally is the fort, which is in a good, defensible condition. The second is my house. For this I stand, and this they did not even venture to attack last year. About the third I will soon speak with you. In addition to this, so that all may be informed as soon as possible, we will establish signals up the river and away from it. For this purpose we must form small squads of troopers which can be rapidly concentrated at threatened points and occupy the enemy until wives and children have accomplished their flight. Cattle, and what else can be concealed, we must secure beforehand. Now, as to what concerns you: It is most likely that this time they will select the creek for attack. They passed by you last year, hence they will hope to find the more with you. And then they know—or believe—that here on the Mohawk we are better prepared and more fully informed than you. The last is probably the case. You live so far off that you could not, upon being pursued, have much prospect of reaching either here or the fort; and for the same reason, we could as little help you. Your father, who was an intelligent man, understood this well, and so strengthened your house that it could for a short time be held by a few well-protected men, furnished with ample provisions and ammunition, against a large troop. On this I have built my plan. You are a good rifleman, and your brother Conrad is the best in the colony. You are both courageous, resolute men, and you have got to carry your own hide to market, which speaks for itself in such circumstances. I will give you two or three men, whom you may yourself select, and it will then be your business to protect yourselves and your neighbors—such as the Ditmars, Teicherts and perhaps also Volzes—who can reach you—Eisenlords and Bellingers are nearer here—until we are in a condition to bring help. I need not tell you, Lambert, upon how responsible and dangerous a post I place you. On your watchfulness hangs not only the life of your neighbors, but perhaps also the fate of all of us about here. On the other hand it may happen that we, with the help of soldiers from Albany, cannot ourselves resist the enemy, and so can either not help you at all, or nct at the right time. Will you, Lambert Sternberg, undertake the charge?"

"I will," said Lambert.

Nicolas Herkimer shook hands with him heartily, and turned to other groups. The minister, who had listened, eagerly twisting his small clothes, and often bowing his head, now reached out his hand to Lambert and said:

"You have not undertaken a small matter, dear young man. May God help you!"

"Amen! honored sir," replied Lambert. "I need your help perhaps more than you are aware of. I came here to make to you a communication, if opportunity offered, highly important to myself, and to ask your advice. Will you listen to me a few minutes? I will try to be brief."

"Speak," said the minister, "though I think I already know what you wish to say."

Lambert looked inquiringly at the minister.

"My dear friend, your Aunt Ditmar has already told me something which I have interpreted according to the disposition of young people. But say on."

Lambert now told the worthy man the history of his love for Catherine from the first moment when he saw her on the deck of the ship to that hour, and at last made known his earnest wish that he might, before all the world, call her his wife.

"I understand, I understand," said the minister, who had been all ears; "yes, yes; for this you may well wish, both on the girl's account and your own; yes, also on account of Conrad, who otherwise might deal some silly blows."

"And so," said Lambert, "as the danger is threatening, I wish as soon as possible to be united to Catherine forever."

"Forever!" said the minister earnestly. "This I also fully understand. Also short and well, dear young friend, I will gladly serve you, as it is my office and my heartfelt wish. We cannot here always observe the forms prescribed by the church, but God sees the heart. So I think to-morrow, satisfied with a single proclamation of the bans, we will attend to the marriage immediately after public worship. Are you satisfied with that? Good; and then I must ask you yet one thing, viz.: That you this evening take the lady to whom you are engaged to your Aunt Ditmar,s and leave her there until to-morrow, and from there bring her to the wedding. I repeat, God looks at the heart, but appearances sway our judgment, and so for the people's sake I wish you would follow my advice."

"I will gladly do it, worthy sir," said Lambert. "I will at once speak to my aunt about it."

"There she comes now," said the minister.

Aunt Ursul had been actively helping Herkimer's women in the house, which the labor of entertaining so many guests at once made necessary. She now declared that, with her consent, not another pitcher of beer or glass of rum should be furnished. "I know my people, and if anything is to come out of the consultation, you must begin now, for an hour hence you might as well preach reason to horses. Say this to Herkimer, dominie. I will look after my old man. You are welcome to go with me, Lambert. He has already asked about you—something that he doesn't do every day. But the French you know bring him into harness. He is to-day quite changed."

Lambert went to his uncle with his aunt, but could not discover any change in him. The old man kept sitting in the same corner on the bench, the fur cap drawn far down on his forehead. His sunken head was scarcely raised in returning Lambert's salutation with a silent nod. However, the otherwise half-closed eyes looked for a moment from under the heavy eyebrows in a peculiar glance, but his thoughts must have wandered far away. He appeared not to hear what Lambert said to him.

"Only let him be," said Aunt Ursul; "he now has other things in his head, and for us it is high time that we at last come to the business. It will likely go like a mixture of cabbage and turnips."

Aunt Ursul appeared to be right. The noise kept increasing. They went around with pitchers and flasks in their hands, and drank to one another, and talked and screamed at each other, till suddenly first one then another shouted: "Still!" "Quiet!" Now the well-known form of the minister appeared, as they crowded through one another. He had climbed on a table and stood there. He had quit turning his snuff-box about in his fingers and waited until they should be ready to listen to him. "Still!" "Quiet!" sounded forth more authoritatively than before. But quiet was not forthcoming. In certain distant groups the loud talking continued, and a coarse voice cried: "What does the dominie want?"

"What I want," called the minister, "I will soon tell you. I beg you, back there, that you will at length keep your mouths shut and bring your wisdom, if you have any, to market at the right time and to the right place."

The rough word awakened laughter everywhere, but after the laughter it became still.

The minister slipped the snuff-box into his pocket,

took off his large three-cornered hat, shoved back the much-used, short wig and thus proceeded:

"I wish with you all to call upon the Lord, and beseech Him that this time the cup, which we emptied last year to the last bitter dregs, the taste of which still lies on our tongues, may graciously pass from us; and if in His incomprehensible wisdom he has decreed that it shall not be so, and that He will again try our hearts and reins, that then, in His grace, He will give us strength to endure the severe trial like brave men who know that the good God, in spite of all and everything, does not forsake him who does not forsake himself, and helps him who helps himself. This, dear friends and countrymen, is a word which has been profitable in many ways and at many times, but never and for no one more than for us at this time. Who will deliver us out of our distress and danger here, on the utmost border of the earth, occupied by people of our race, where surrounding enemies lurk and go about to destroy us, but God and ourselves? And with God's help we will save ourselves—of this I am fully convinced—if we keep His commandment which reads: 'Thou shalt love thy neighbor as thyself.' Since if we, as it becomes neighbors, stand beside each other, shoulder to shoulder, with one mind and one heart, and full of the same courage in danger, distress and death, then and only then, dear friends, shall we overcome the danger and deliver ourselves from the distress, and die, should death meet us, as brave men, discharging our highest duty as men and Christians. And now, dear friends, after having said what I, as a servant of the Word of God and a man of peace, wished to say, from a full and loving heart, I thank you that you have listened to me attentively. Will you not with equal attention listen to the man whom we all know and honor, an honest farmer like yourselves, and in addition a brave soldier. May the Lord bless him so that he may give you good advice; and may the Lord bless you so that you may take advice; and may He protect us all and let the light cf His countenance fall upon us and give us peace. Amen."

The earnest words of the minister, who spoke—especially toward the last—with a deeply moved voice, did not entirely fail of their effect. An approving murmur ran here and there through the assembly. But the voice of the speaker had scarcely ceased and his form disappeared from the table when again, though not as loud as before, some voices were raised asking what was the object of the talk? whether they had come here to hear a sermon?

"Talking costs no money and the minister can talk well. He was last year one of the first to run for the fort, and left the rest to their fate, but truly it is well not to be before a gun when it is fired off."

So here and there spake those who were dissatisfied. Others said they should be ashamed to say such things about so excellent a man. Others called:

"Quiet! don't you see that Herkimer wants to speak?"

So at last Nicolas Herkimer, who had already stood on the table a few minutes and let his keen, earnest eyes pass over the assembly, raised his voice. He spoke long and impressively. He unfolded in every particular the plan which he had, in its chief parts, before told Lambert. In it he had thought of every-thing, remembered everything, and reduced to its smallest compass the threatened danger that could be avoided.

"That is what I have to say," he concluded. "Now it is for you to test my proposals. We are free men, and each one can in the end do what he pleases, and carry his hide to market this way or that. But that we are free does not forbid us to be united. On the other hand, only by being united shall we preserve and protect our freedom. United we cannot be and become, if you talk and cry out among each other as just now you did, again. Whoever knows anything better than I, let him come here and speak. Let him who does not, keep still and listen. And let us not forget—what we tell our children—that he who will not hear must feel. Who wishes to speak after me?"

"I!" "I!" called out a couple of dozen voices.

"You cannot all speak at once," said Herkimer with some bitterness; "so you come here, Hans Haberkorn. You screamed the loudest."

Hans Haberkorn, the ferryman, appeared beside Herkimer on the table. The small, undersized, barefoot fellow who had, behind the bar connected with his ferry, so often spoken large words and scolded his rich neighbor on the other side of the river, could not let the opportunity pass to tell the last speaker the truth—as he expressed it—before all the world. He wanted to know whether it was honest and neighborly in Nicolas Herkimer that he wanted three ferries at the same time over the river within half a mile of each other, after it had been promised him, Hans Haberkorn, that he should be the only ferryman on this ground? That he on that account had settled on a piece of land which consisted of moor and sand, and on which he would long since have starved if he had not also a beer saloon. Now the two ferries should be used only in urgent cases, and then again discontinued, or—what would follow—let the wolf eat. It was absolutely certain that one ferry without a beer saloon could not support itself. Both the other ferries would want to set up beer saloons, and then it would be to him, personally, the same whether the French came to-day or to-morrow and killed him with his wife and children. For his part he would rather be put to death at once than starve to death by degrees.

"Hans Haberkorn is right!" called out half a dozen voices.

"Shame on the good-for-nothing fellow who thinks only about himself!" cried others, and pressed toward the table from which Hans Haberkorn quickly jumped.

The place he vacated was again occupied by big John
Mertens, who had a large farm on the moor between
the Mohawk and the creek, near the church, and by
some was considered to be better off than Herkimer
himself.   In any case one could always be sure that
John Mertens would oppose anything that Herkimer
and the minister wanted, of whom he observed that
they always stuck under the same cover.   With this
—his favorite expression—he began his ´discourse,
saying: That one might well know what to think of
a plan that had been formed without consulting him,
John Mertens, who also had a word to say, having
ten head of cattle in the pasture more than people
whom he would not name; nor would he speak of
the sheep and the English hogs which he had first
introduced; that every child knew that one could not
bring sheep out of a stable when the roof over their
heads was afire; nor could one drive fifty hogs away
so fast that a lame Indian could not overtake them,
not to speak of a dozen who could run.   They might
think of John Mertens so or so, but he is an honest
fellow who does not hide his meaning behind a bush.
This was what he wanted to say—The discourse of
the big farmer was very confused, and was partly lost
in the fat of his double chin; but his adherents, of
whom the number was not small, showed their appro-
bation with screams and yells.   The opposite party
did not fail to pay back such an answer as was due.
A dreadful tumult arose, which Nicolas Herkimer's

powerful voice could not overcome. It seemed as if
the consultation on whose issue the weal or woe of
hundreds hung, through the folly and conceit of a
couple of dozen would end in empty confusion and
disorder.

Suddenly there stood beside Nicolas Herkimer a
person, the mere sight of whom, as with a blow,
brought the boisterous assembly to order, as though a
dead man had become alive and wished to address
them. The giant-long, skeleton-lean form of Christian Ditmar, whose bony hands were stretched apart
as if in conjuration, while, from under the thick fur
cap the gray hair in disordered strands was whipped
by the wind about his ghost-like face, was awe-inspir-
ing. Then he raised his voice, which now shrieked
frantically, and then again rung out like thunder, and
thus spoke:

"So is being fulfilled the Word of God: 'The sins
of the fathers shall be visited upon the children to the
third and fourth generation.' Yes, the sins of the
fathers. You have quarreled with each other and
raised your arms against each other while French
wolves are howling around the German flock, and
have worried and killed as their wicked hearts desired.
They murdered my parents and brothers and sisters.
I saw it with my own eyes. I saw too my parents'
house go up in flames, and our neighbors' houses
burning, and the city became a ruin and an ash-heap
—the beautiful proud city on the Neckar. Among

the ruins wandered weeping wives looking among the ashes for the bones of husbands and brothers, and cried: 'Woe!' 'Woe!' 'A deadly curse on you hangmen and murdering incendiaries!'

"I, a weak boy, cried along with them: 'Woe! Woe! A curse upon you, you hangmen, and murdering incendiaries!' After many years I came here, and again found them, the mean French wolves, howling around the German flock; and I disputed with the rest and separated from the others, and went out with my wife and my sons to take vengeance on those who had killed my parents and all my kindred. How did the vengeance look when my four brave boys lay dead at their father's feet, each with a bullet through his breast?"

Christian Ditmar was silent a few moments. He must suppress the sadness that rose in his heart at these recollections. He then proceeded with increasing emotion:

"And so you have suffered and bled, earlier and later, under the greedy teeth. However I, who have suffered more than you all, I tell you that I deserved it since I blindly followed the voice of my heart crying for vengeance and did not hearken to the advice of more prudent men; and so you have deservedly suffered, and will suffer, since you also will not listen, you fools and madmen, and propose to separate as you came, the one this way, the other that, by which the wolves will again have an easy play. But then

your own and your children's blood will rest on you
as my children's blood has come upon me.   Here—!"

Christian Ditmar tore his fur cap from his head.
A broad, fearful scar ran like a stream of blood over
the high forehead from one temple to the other.

"Here!" he repeated, while with his forefinger he
pointed to the track of blood; "here! here!"   He
raised both hands to his head, and with a dull cry that
rang dreadfully through the silent assembly, he fell
helpless.   Nicolas Herkimer caught him in his arms;
but soon the old man gathered himself up and, with
Lambert's help, who quickly sprang to his aid, descended from the table and walked slowly to the entrance into the door-yard, supported by the strong
arm of his wife and attended by Lambert.

"Have you now heard?" said Aunt Ursul to the
rest who crowded around, helpful and eager.   "Have
you now heard, you straw-heads?   Why do you stand
about here and gape?   I can take care of my old
man alone.   Better go and do what he has told you.
You also stay here, Lambert, and when you pass our
house stop a moment.   I wish to speak with you."

Lambert brought out the horses of his relatives
from the long row of those which were swinging their
tails under the shed, and bridled them.   He now
helped into the saddle his uncle, who had fallen back
into his former stupidity, and after his great excitement seemed to take no farther part in the matter.
Meanwhile Aunt Ursul had resolutely brought a stool

and from it mounted her horse. Lambert looked at the retreating figures until they reached the ferry, where Hans Haberkorn's oldest boy, in the absence of his father, attended to the service, and then returned to the meeting, in which there now prevailed a very different mood.

The appearance and words of Christian Ditmar had produced a powerful effect. Everybody knew the witless Christian and his history, and that he had been dumb since he had lost his sons, and his oldest friends could no longer remember the sound of his voice. And now the dumb had opened his mouth and had spoken fearful words, which cut to the heart those who listened in dumb wonderment. Yes, yes; it was, if not a miracle, at least a sign—a gray sign —well enough understood by the superstitious. When men are silent stones will speak. They had not been silent before—far otherwise—but they had not listened; they would now listen; they wanted to hear Herkimer explain his views once more.

Nicolas Herkimer did so, and with a result far different from the first. They now found that it must be altogether so, and not otherwise—that better advice could not be given. Should the French this time select Canada Creek as the first point of attack, as to all appearance they would, it would be very bad for Lambert Sternberg and the Ditmars and the Eisenlords and the rest. But it could not be helped. When now Lambert appeared on the table and in a

few plain words said that he was proud to assume
the existing responsibility, and tha the would hold out
on his post to his last breath, and that he now desired the young men who had a heart and a good rifle
for the undertaking, at once to go with him to-day;
then August and Fritz Volz and Christian Eisenlord,
and half a dozen others, cried out: "I!" "I!" with
one voice, and pressing up joined the fighting band.

The leaders of the three cavalry squads were now
selected. These were to help those on and away
from the Mohawk, and on the creek, as they were flee-
ing to the forts. So also right men were quickly appointed for the old ferry, and for the added new ones,
and for the other important posts which were yet to
be provided for.

The excellent spirit which had seized the assembly
made them unwilling to hear any more quarreling and
strife; and those who grumbled secretly, such as Hans
Haberkorn, John Mertens and others, thought it better policy to lay aside their opposition for a more con-
venient time.

It was late in the afternoon when Nicolas Herkimer
declared the business finished, and asked the minister to close the meeting. The minister put up his
snuff-box, stepped on the table and spoke with a loud
voice which clearly indicated deep feeling, as follows:

"Dear neighbors and friends: I will not speak long,
for you are in a hurry to get home to your wives and
children. I will only ask you with me briefly to thank

God that He has opened our hearts to the spirit of
brotherliness and love, and to beseech Him that He
will keep awake in us this spirit for the miserable
days with which we are now threatened. Then this
open heart and this wakeful spirit will make our hands
strong, and we shall live in a strong tower, which is
our God. And the prince of this world, however terrible he may be, will accomplish nothing against the
eternal God in heaven, who will not leave His brave
Germans. And now, dear neighbors and friends, go
home, and keep your eyes stiff and your powder dry.
To-morrow, as may happen, if you have more to do
and cannot come to church, no damage will be done.
God give us all a happy reunion. Amen."

"Amen!" Amen!" sounded forth everywhere in
the circle of men, among whom there were none who
had not found for the moment a deep and holy earnestness. They had assembled in disputation and
quarreling. They separated in peace and harmony.
Most of them at their departure went to shake hands
with Nicolas Herkimer, and specially assured him
that he could in any case rely on them. The honor
of a pinch of snuff from the minister was sought by
so many that the noble man could at last, laughing,
only present the empty box. The young people who
desired to be placed on the most dangerous post, had
gathered about Lambert, and it required Herkimer's
authority to settle the choice. Lambert had declared
that he could not accept more than four, since he

himself and Conrad must also be added, making six good rifles for the protection of the house. A larger number would unnecessarily consume food and ammunition in case they had to stand a siege. So then, to grieve no one, the lot should determine, and it fell on Fritz Volz, from the creek; Jacob Ehrlich and Anthony Bierman, from the Mohawk; and on Richard Herkimer. Lambert was satisfied with the issue. They were, on the whole, wide-awake young men— at least Fritz Volz and Richard Herkimer, his special friends. They agreed that the last two, who lived near enough, should occupy the post yet this evening, and that the two others should come early in the morning.

Now at last, after about all who had been assembled had gone, could Lambert leave Nicolas Herkimer, who said: "I will keep you no longer now. I will ride over to-morrow, as there are yet many things about which I want to talk to you." Lambert had not improperly pressed to go. As he reached the other side he found the Eisenlords, the Teicherts and a dozen others who all, with a glass of Hans Haberkorn's genuine, were discussing what they had heard and decided upon. He shook hands with them and hastened on, Fritz Volz calling after him that he would see him in the evening. As now he gave loose rein to his horse he cast an anxious, inquiring glance at the sky, in which the sun had nearly run its course. It was perhaps yet half an hour to its setting. On his left the level fields and marshes shimmered and glimmered in red, blended lights, so that he could hardly distinguish the shingled roofs of the houses; and the forms of riders and footmen appeared now and then as dark points in the sea of fire. To the right, where the farther he went the nearer did the hills and rocks press toward him, the mighty trunks of the giant pines glowed in dark purple, and their branching tops blazed in green-golden flames to the cloudless sky. With every hoof-beat of the horse the sun sunk deeper, and Lambert had just left Bellinger's farm behind when the sea of fire to the left was extinguished by a blue fog; and toward evening only the highest tops of the tallest trees reflected the departing light of day. Night soon came on. As his noble beast rapidly struck the grassy soil with strong hoofs he saw that he could not reach home in less than an hour.

A nameless discontent seized him. The longing for the beloved one, which he had so nobly fought all these hours, now asserted its rights, and so filled his breast that he could hardly breathe. Minutes seemed like hours. There was also another distressing feeling—a feeling of fear for something he could not conceive of, for which he had no name, and which may on that account have been more terrible. In all his life he had never before had such an experience. Nearest to it were the frightful dreams that had terrified him when a boy, from which he in vain sought to wake. Lambert groaned aloud, and Hans groaned under the pressure of the rider's legs.

So he rushed forward faster and faster, without looking to the right or left, without stopping at Eisenlord's or at Volz', though everywhere from the doors the women called to him: "Holla, Lambert, whither in such haste?" until at last Hans, angry at the conduct of his otherwise reasonable master, ran at full speed.

Aunt Ursul had requested him to stop on his return, and he himself wished to speak with her about what the minister had said. So he stopped his foaming horse unwillingly when he came to the Ditmar house.

"Is he near comfort?" said Aunt Ursul who had heard him coming and now stepped to the door. "The poor beast is like a cat which has been lying eight days in the water. How you look yourself: Like the rider in the book of Revelation."

"I feel as though some misfortune had happened there," stammered Lambert, pointing homeward.

"Päpperlapap!" said Aunt Ursul. "What can have happened? Conrad—yes, Lambert;. I already see that now I can't get a rational word out of you, so in God's name, drive on. I have just put my old man to bed and given him a cup of tea, so I am entirely free and will come over in about an hour."

She gave Hans, who was already restlessly champing his bit, a blow on his wet neck. He sprang away with his rider. "Those whom we love are always but half near comfort," said Aunt Ursul, looking after him and shaking her head; "nevertheless—nevertheless—Conrad is a madcap, and acted this morning as though he had lost his reason.   I must see that all things go right."

Aunt Ursul turned back into the house, took her gun from the rack and, with long strides, followed Lambert, who was already immersed in thé evening fog which rose from the creek in thick streaks.

CHAPTER X

When at noon to-day Lambert tore himself away from Catherine, she stood still as though stunned. The conviction that she ought to remain behind had come to her on the instant; the determination to do so had been uttered so soon; the carrying out of the resolution too had followed so closely at its heels, that now, as the forms of the riders disappeared behind a turn of the road and she found herself really alone, it appeared to her as though she were having a disagreeable, fearful dream out of which she must momentarily awake. She struck herself over her forehead and eyes, but all was real. There stood the empty crib. There lay the pail which the mare had pushed over. There was the pillion which at the last moment Lambert had unbuckled from the saddle. There were the short, trampled grass and the tracks of the hoofs of the horses. There was the open door in which she had just now seen Lambert. Catherine took a few steps, as though she would follow the beloved one, and then stood still, pressing her hand on her loud-beating heart. Deep sadness overwhelmed her, but she vigorously fought down the feeling. "He has so often called you a brave girl," said she to herself, "and will you weep and complain like a child

137

which the mother has left alone for a few moments? He will soon come back; surely he will soon come back."

She entered the house to see what time it was. The hand of the Swartzwald clock pointed to twelve. The distance to Nicolas Herkimer's house was six miles. If she counted going and returning it was twelve, and on the calculation of the men themselves would take them two hours, so that Lambert could be back by six o'clock, or by seven at the latest. That was indeed a long time, but there was yet much to do, and perhaps also to-day Conrad would return earlier from hunting.

"On Conrad's account I should remain here," said Catherine to herself as she cleared away the dinner-dishes. "He must learn to see in me his sister, and he will, when we show our confidence in him and have no secrets before him. Ah, could I only yesterday have greeted him as a brother! However, that will follow. It must follow yet to-day, when he returns. Then we will live together in peace, and the wild man will find that it is not a bad thing to have a female friend who takes care of him until he himself loves a girl, and establishes a home and builds a house for himself here near us, or at the edge of the woods he so much loves. That will be a joyful, happy life. We will be good neighbors. I shall love his wife and she me."

Catherine had sat down on the hearth and, with

her head supported by her hand, looked before her
with half-closed eyes, thinking. The fire on the
hearth gently crackled; the wall-clock said "tick-tack."
In the meadow outside the birds sang. Through the
open door the sun shone clear into the cool, shaded
room; and in the bright sunbeams, which reached as
far as her knees, dust atoms danced, lighted up, and
twinkling like golden stars seemed to be waving and
playing and catching one another. Then they were
no longer golden stars, but children's laughing faces,
which emerged out of the partial darkness of the back-
ground, came up to her knees, and again disappeared
in the dark corners, and from them looked out with
bright, blue, happy eyes. Then the vision vanished.
The sun still shone into the silent room. The fire
crackled. The wall-clock said "tick-tack," and out
in the meadows sang the birds.

The young maiden arose and commenced her
labor anew, but there was a different expression in
her mild, innocent countenance; and other thoughts,
which came to her like a revelation, filled her soul.
The bridal feeling which now happified her, had
acquired another phase, for which she knew not how
to account. It was a deeper, more earnest feeling—
distinguished from the former like the light of noon
now lying on field and forest, from that of the morning. Those were the same bending grass-stems and
the same swaying tree-tops. It was the same clear
creek and they were the same waving rushes, and

yet all was changed as by a gentle, mighty, magic hand, and spoke another speech—moving and dissolving in mystery. Now she understood why the beloved man, who was truth and openness itself, so anxiously concealed from her for weeks that she must live alone with him in his house. "Alone! Would it not have been the same had he told the truth? told me that he loved me? that he did not want me as a maid-servant? Would it not have come out just the same? Did I not also love him from the first moment on? and have I not followed him through peopled cities, through the pathless wilderness, on a journey of weeks, through rain and sunshine, day and night, in unknown regions? What is so different now? Did I not devote myself to him as we left the ship hand in hand? 'You shall be my lord!' And is it not said in the church when the minister lays the hands of lovers together: 'He shall be thy lord.' Yes, he shall be my lord, now and always. He shall be my lord."

So spoke Catherine to herself to banish the occasional shudders that passed through her heart and often took away her breath, while she completed the arrangements in her room which had been tempora · rily made last evening, and put away her few belongings in a closet that had been contrived in the thick wall. Then, as there was nothing more to do here, she for the first time ascended the stairs to the upper story, and walked around the gallery which encircled

the house and projected beyond the lower story, and
was surrounded by well-joined planks and provided
with port-holes. With the exception of a place
poorly enough partitioned off in which the brothers
had slept the previous night, the room, used in winter
as a store-room, was empty, or served for the storage
of that for which there was no room below. Catherine acquired a clearer notion of the plan, which she
and Lambert had formed in the morning, to prepare
a small, pleasant room for them both here where
everything was more airy and free. However, without Lambert she did not succeed very well in plan-
ning.

So she again went downstairs, and to her surprise
saw by the clock that since Lambert had left but one
hour had elapsed. She took some work and seated
herself with it on a bench before the door in the shade
of the gallery.

It was in the stillness of the day. There was so
little wind that the grass-stems in the meadow, and
the rushes at the edge of the creek, scarcely bent.
The butterflies passed from flower to flower on languid wing. The hum of the bees and the chirping of
the crickets had a sleepy sound. All around, everything was still. However, out of the forest there
frequently came the hoarse cry of the tree-falcon, or
the call of a bird which Catherine did not recognize.
In the blue sky there hung single white clouds whose
shadows moved, slowly—very slowly—over the sunny
prairie.

At first Catherine was pleased with this quietude, which seemed an image of sabbath stillness, filling her soul. But she had scarcely thus sat an hour be-- fore the monotony of the scene about her filled her heart with a strange fear. How entirely different it was this morning. Then heaven and earth and tree and bush and every flower and every grass-stem smiled and bowed their welcome to her. Every- thing had spoken to her in persuasive language. Now that the beloved one was at a distance everything was dumb, except that heaven and earth and tree and bush and every flower and every grass-stem breathed out one word with ever-increasing sadness: Alone! alone!

Catherine let her work sink into her lap. An image, that had been for many years as if blotted from her memory, suddenly came before her in pale colors, but very distinct—the image of her dead mother, who, adorned with flowers, lay in her coffin —and she a little girl, ten years old, stood beside it; and her father had come up and taken her hand and said: "We two are now alone."

"Alone!"

Her heart was filled with increasing fear. Again taking up her work she tried to sing a song that always occurred to her when everything was so quiet: "Were I a wild Falcon I would soar aloft." But she commenced so gently that she did not complete the first measure. Her voice sounded strange. She was frightened at her own voice.

Perhaps, she thought, it would be better if she went to the barn-yard where in the morning she had passed such happy moments with Lambert.

She arose and hastily walked down the path, at last running, and now with beating heart leaned against the bars of the inclosure. The sheep which stood near ran away frightened, and looked at her from a distance with dull eyes. In the yard all was still. The hens and turkeys had gone out into the fields. As she again turned, from among the fruit trees, in whose blossom-covered branches this morning a robin sang so sweetly, there broke out a brown bird of prey and with broad, flapping wings hastened toward the forest. On the ground among the grass there lay several colored feathers.

More sad than when she went Catherine returned to the house, and again sat down before the door, with the full purpose now to wait quietly, and to fight down her depression of spirits.

So she sat patiently long, endless hours. The light in the green tops of the trees in yonder woods became more golden. The shadows that lay along the edge became deeper and broader—one after another came out of the wilderness until at last they branched out in troops. From time to time flocks of pigeons flew like lightning over the prairie from one side of the forest to the other. High above them, in the bright sky, sailed more slowly chains of wild geese, filling the air with their monotone cry. Then again everything was still, and Catherine could hear the rushing of the blood in her temples.

She could endure it no longer. It occurred to her that she had seen a couple of books in the house on a shelf too high for her to reach. She went in, pushed up the table, set a stool on it and got the books.

There were two of them, bound in hog's leather, very dusty and worm-eaten—a Bible and a history, as it appeared. The writing on the fly-leaf was at first in Latin, which the minister's daughter understood well enough to deciper with a little pains. It stated that this book belonged to Conrad Emanuel Sternberg, formerly a student of theology at Heidelberg, who, in the year 1709, after his parents—well-to-do vintners in the Palatinate—had lost everything in the dreadful winter, when the wine in the casks and the birds in the air froze, in company with the young cooper, Christian Ditmar, from Heidelberg, had determined upon the great undertaking of emigrating to America, which he reached June 13th, 1710, more dead than alive, after a long and tedious voyage from the Rhine through Holland and by way of England. He settled on the Hudson with his friends and fellow-sufferers, where he hoped to end his life in quietness and peace.

This pious wish was not fulfilled. Further notices followed this connected narrative, but written in the German language, as though the writer had mean-

while forgotten his Latin, saying that he had moved
with his faithful companion, Christian Ditmar, from
the Hudson to the Mohawk, thence to Schoharie and
finally to Canada Creek. Then there was the date
of his marriage with Elisabeth Christiane Frank, of
Schoharie, the younger sister of Ursula, his old friend's
and now brother-in-law's wife, the birthdays of his
sons, Lambert and Conrad, and the death of Christiane. With this sad event the record of the life of
the old Heidelberg student was closed. He had not
written a line more.

Catherine looked thoughtfully at the faded writing,
gently closed the lid and opened the second, smaller
book. It was entitled: "Description of the destruction of the city of Heidelberg on the 22nd and 23rd
of May, 1689."

She began to read mechanically until by degrees
she became conscious of what she was reading and
sprang up with a dull outcry: "Great God! what
have I read? Is it possible that human beings can so
rage against one another - that there are tyrants to
whom neither the silvered hair of the aged, nor the
modesty of the maiden, nor the innocent laughter of
children—to whom nothing is sacred?

"Why not? Did not the bands under Soubise
ravage through the cities and towns of Hanover? And
did not their ruthless cruelty and base shamelessness
drive her old father and all her neighbors and friends
from their beloved homes across the sea? Were they

not the sons and grandsons of those robbers who, under Melac and Borges, burnt the Palatinate and reduced Heidelberg to a dust heap?

"And again, did they not, the year before, ravage here just so, in connection with the Indians, their like-minded confederates? Here, among these hills and in these valleys and woods, the same French were threatening again and their approach was already proclaimed. Dreadful! dreadful!"

The poor girl, though so sore and sad at heart, had up to this moment found no definite cause of fear. Now fear overwhelmed her with sudden power. She looked with fixed eyes toward the edge of the forest as though at every moment the French and Indians were about to break forth from its silent recesses. She listened intently, until the blood seemed to boil in her temples, and as though it would burst the veins. Merciful God! What would become of her? How could Lambert leave her in such a howling wilderness?—he who had so long been her guardian and defense—he who had cherished her as the apple of his eye. If only Conrad would come. It was about the same time yesterday when he came—no, it was later; the sun had already set, and now it was still over the woods. But why should he to-day stay out so long? And who, besides Lambert, could better protect her than Lambert's brother, the strong, alert man who only needed to set his foot across the door-step to make those dwelling in the house feel secure? So

Lambert said only this morning. Why did he now stay away when his presence was so much desired?

Catherine pressed her hands against her beating temples. What should she do? What could she do but wait and try to hush a fear that surely was childish. There near her lay the Bible. She had so often, in sad hours, drawn from it rest and comfort. She took it up and read where her eyes happened to fall:

"And the Lord had respect unto Abel and to his offering. But unto Cain and his offering he had not respect. And Cain was very wroth and his countenance fell. And the Lord said unto Cain: Why art thou wroth? and why is thy countenance fallen? * * * And Cain talked with his brother Abel, and it came to pass when they were in the field, Cain rose up against Abel his brother and slew him."

The printed page glimmered before her eyes. With a dull cry the affrighted girl sprang up. "Cain killed Abel! Cain killed Abel!" And she had wished that he—the terrible one—were here—he who this morning had uttered such dreadful threatenings. No, no! he must not come back; he must not find her alone. He must not see her again. She must away to meet Lambert. She must warn him—must tell him that his brother would kill him on her account; that he must give her up, or with her go out into the wide world. They must flee from the brother. He must save her and himself from that dreaded brother.

As though the block-house was on fire Catherine

hastened from the door, down the hill, to the creek, along the creek, without looking around, without observing that she had started in the opposite direction so that at every step she was farther away from Lambert. When she reached the bridge where Lambert had yesterday overtaken her she became aware of her mistake. But she was like a wrecked vessel driven shoreward by the waves and then again carried out to sea. Destruction by him from whom she would escape seemed unavoidable. No more capable of forming a further purpose, deprived of all strength, she sunk together; and as though she must here await the expected death-blow, she bowed her head and covered her face with her hands.

"Catherine!"

Slowly she withdrew her hands from her deadly pale face, and saw Conrad standing before her with his rifle on his shoulder and his dog at his heels, looking at her with vacant eyes, and appearing to have just come out of the sedge along the shore. She had anticipated his coming—knew that he would come. She no longer felt that nameless dread. On the other hand there instantly came over her a peculiar restfulness, and in a quiet tone she said: "You come late. I have been waiting for you."

"Indeed?" said Conrad.

He was also very pale, and the expression of his face was strangely changed.

Catherine observed it, but it could not change her

purpose to proceed, even should it cost her life. She arose from her reclining position, though not without an effort—her limbs seemed as if dead—and, as she began mechanically to return to the house, she said:

"I have been waiting for you, since I wish to say something to you before I leave your house."

Conrad started. Catherine felt it, though she kept her eyes directed to the ground. However, involuntarily walking faster, she proceeded:

"What I could not tell you this morning, for it has taken place since, I will say now. I have become engaged to your brother."

She expected that now an outbreak would follow, but Conrad walked on silently at her side.

"I engaged myself to him," said Catherine—and her voice became firmer while she spoke—"this morning after you were gone, and I hardly know how it came about. I only know that Lambert has done for me more than any other man, excepting my good old father who is dead; that to him I owe my life, which therefore belongs to him; that at any time he might ask for it he might have it of me. He did not ask it of me this morning, but I gave it to him freely —my life and my love—for that is the same. And now—"

"And now?" asked Conrad.

"Now I must away, if you are not the kind brother whom Lambert loves so much—if you are resolved to turn the angry words you spoke this morning into fierce deeds. How could I remain here and see how I have sown strife between brother and brother, especially at this time, when you should stand shoulder to shoulder against the treacherous enemy? Where I shall go I do not know. I only know that I cannot stay, so long as you are angry at your brother on my account. But, Conrad, while I thus speak, it seems to me entirely impossible that you can place yourself between me and your brother."

"Why impossible?" asked Conrad.

"Because you love your brother," replied Catherine, gathering courage as she spoke. "You have every reason to love him, though you do not love me as Lambert loves me. Why should you? You do not know me. You saw me yesterday for the first time, and a few minutes this morning. Though I may indeed have pleased you, yet, as you now hear that my heart is already given to your brother, what else, as an honorable man, can you do than to rejoice at our happiness as we would rejoice in yours should heaven provide you a similar happiness, which I hope may soon happen?"

They had reached the house. The dog, which with long leaps had gone ahead, met them wagging her tail and springing against her master   Conrad pushed the animal away, but not with his usual rough force. His manner was more sad than angry and his motions were like those of one who is very tired. He sank down on the bench on which Catherine's work and the books still lay, supported his elbow on his knee and rested his head on his hand.

"You are hungry and thirsty from your long hunt," said Catherine; "shall I prepare your evening meal?"

Conrad shook his head. All fear had vanished from Catherine's soul. As she saw the wild, intractable man sitting there so still—so sunk within himself—there stirred in her heart stronger and stronger another feeling.

"Conrad," said she softly. "Conrad," she repeated, laying her hand on his shoulder, "I will indeed also hold you very dear."

A dull cry, like that of an animal that has been mortally wounded, broke from Conrad's broad chest. He put both hands to his face and wept aloud like a child, and the body of the giant-like man shook from the pain stirring within him as might the small frame of a child.

Catherine for a moment stood helpless and speechless. Then there also came from her eyes warm tears, and with the tears she found words—mild, kind words—of sympathy and comfort. She told him again and again that she would love him as a sister should love a brother; that his young, sorrowful heart would find peace; that he should see in her his sister; and that he would find pure happiness in this feeling until there blossomed out another happiness in the love of a virtuous girl, in which no one would more deeply share than she and Lambert.

"Do not speak his name," said Conrad.

He had jumped up, all his limbs shaking with anger and his eyes flashing. He convulsively grasped his gun, which stood near, by the barrel.

"You think you are going to play me off with words. For me smooth words; for him kisses! I saw to-day in the woods how handsomely you can kiss."

He broke out in loud laughter. Catherine, frightened, drew back.

"So!" said Conrad, "that is your true face. Do you still love me as a sister her brother?"

"If you are so unbrotherly, no!" said Catherine. "But you do not know what you are saying."

"Truly not," growled Conrad.

"And not what you are doing," said Catherine. "You would otherwise be ashamed to torment a poor, helpless girl."

She leaned against the door-post, pale and trembling, her hands folded over her breast, her large eyes fixed on the angry man, who tried in vain to meet her gaze, and raved before her like a wild animal.

Then the dog dashed forward, and at the same moment the dull hoof-beats of a horse in full run became perceptible. Fear seized Catherine as to what the issue would be should Lambert now return—and it could be no other.

"Conrad!" she called; "Conrad, it is your brother."

Impelled by an overwhelming feeling she threw

herself before him and wound her arms about his knees.

"Let me be!" cried Conrad.

"Not till you have sworn that you will not injure him."

"Let me be!" cried Conrad again, and he violently tore her loose. Catherine tottered forward, stumbled and fell. Her head struck hard against the door-sill.

She came near fainting, but with a great effort picked herself up again, as angry voices struck her ear, and threw herself between the brothers.

"Lambert! Conrad! For God's sake, rather kill me! Conrad, it is your brother. Lambert, he does not know what he is doing!"

The brothers released each other. and panting, looked at one another with flashing eyes. By the sound Lambert's rifle had fallen to the ground. Conrad held his half-raised in his strong hands.

"Now," said Lambert; "why do you not shoot?"

"I do not want to kill you," said Conrad. "If I wanted your life I could have taken it this morning."

"What then do you want?"

"Nothing from you. Why did you come just now? You shall not see me again. Since we have happened again to meet, let me tell you that it must be the last time. Go your own way and let me go mine."

With a powerful swing he threw his rifle on his shoulder and turned away.

Lambert intercepted him. "You must not go. I

will forget that you raised your hand against me.   Do
you also forget that I raised mine against you.   By
the memory of our father; by the memory of our
mother, I conjure you, do not leave your parents'
house."

"It is too small for us all," said Conrad, with bitter scorn.

"Then *we* will leave it.   I will gladly do it if you
will but stay."

"I need no house," said Conrad.

"The house, however, needs you, as you can help
defend it against our bitter enemies.   Do you wish to
see it go up in flames?   You know that the French
are coming—perhaps you know more about it than I
—than all of us; and we to-day greatly missed you.
Will you become a traitor to our common interests
—to your brother, your friends, to wives and children?   Conrad, you must not go away!"

"If the enemy comes you will again creep away as
you did before," said Conrad.   "I will not hide in
forts.   I will fight openly.   I will take the matter in
hand entirely alone, and you may here, in your holes,
go to destruction or not; it will not trouble me.   My
blood be upon me if I again set either foot across this
door-sill!"

He pushed his fur cap down over his eyes, whistled
to his dog, and as he, making his rounds about the
house, did not come, he called out:

"So you, too, stay here.   Curse on you all!"

That was the last word that Catherine heard. The dreadful, soul-stirring excitement of these hours had exhausted her strength, and her fall had broken her down entirely. She felt a stinging pain in her temples. There was a ringing in her ears. She saw Lambert's form, as through a veil, bending over her; and then it was not Lambert, but Aunt Ursul, and then everything sunk away about her in deep night.

CHAPTER XI

Aunt Ursul sat at Catherine's bed in the room carefully noticing every motion of the young girl who lay there, pale, with closed eyes, half asleep as it appeared. She repeatedly felt her pulse, and renewed the cold cloths on her forehead. She then again bent over her, listened to her quiet breathing, then bowed satisfied and murmured: "There's nothing more to be done here now. We will now look after the young man."

She arose and retired, as quietly as her heavy boots would permit, from the chamber, her face expressing displeasure as the door creaked a little, though she shut it very softly. Lambert, who had been sitting at the hearth, raised his head and looked at her who was entering with anxious eye. Aunt Ursul sat down by his side, placed her feet firmly on the hearth, and said, in a tone intended to be a whisper, but on account of her deep, rough voice was a dull growl:

"No, Lambert, on that side"—she at the same time inclined her large head toward the chamber—"so far it goes quite well. The girl is a brave child, and will to-morrow again stand firm in her shoes. If we women should at once discover your stupidities we would have much to do."

Lambert seized the hand of the kind woman. Tears stood in his eyes. Aunt Ursul did not know how it happened, but her eyelashes also became moist. She breathed deeply two or three times, and said: "You ought to be ashamed, Lambert. You really have a heart like a young chicken, and now it occurs to me that I have eaten nothing the whole day. Give me a piece of bread and some ham, or whatever you have, and if there is yet a swallow of rum in the flask it won't do any hurt—but add to it two-thirds water. A well-behaved person will not otherwise drink the fiery stuff. And now we will once have a little rational talk, Lambert. We need not be in a hurry. The girl sleeps so soundly that she will not wake under six hours."

Lambert had taken what was wanted out of the cupboard. Aunt Ursul moved her chair to the table, and while she was eating heartily, said:

"Do you know, Lambert, that the girl is a treasure?"

Lambert bowed.

"And that neither you, nor Conrad, nor any man in this earthly vale of tears, is good enough for the maiden?"

Lambert's eyes said: "Yes."

"I have now for the first time carefully looked at her," said Aunt Ursul; "as she lay there, white and bloody, like the doves this morning. There is not

one false or distorted line in her lovely face. Everything is entire purity and innocence, as though the
Lord God had opened a window in heaven and sent
her forth upon the earth. And now to think that such
a lovely angel is destined to all the suffering and an-
guish which is our inheritance from our mother Eve
—Good God, it is dreadful! Since, rightly considered, Lambert, you cannot help it, as you did not
make the world, and are all in all a good man, Lambert—yes, a right good man— what Aunt Ursul can
do to smooth the way to your happiness that she will
do with all her heart. Yes, surely, Lambert, that she
will."

"I thank you, aunt," replied Lambert. "I can
truly say that I have always been persuaded of your
good will, and have constantly reckoned on you, but
I am afraid that now nobody can any longer help us.
How shall I stand with her before God's altar when I
know that my brother begrudges me my happiness?
Even could I do so, Catherine could not bear the
thought that it is she on whose account Conrad is
irreconcilably angry. She knows how I have loved
the young man—how I still love him. I could shed
my blood for him, and how did he renounce us even
now—even now?"

Lambert supported his forehead with his hand.
On Aunt Ursul's rough face there also lay a deep,
helpless sadness. She wished to say something comforting to Lambert, but found nothing to say. Lambert proceeded:

"I am not angry at him. How could I be? You know, aunt, that we were long uncertain whether he or I should go to New York, since he had less to keep him, and we thought it would do him good to get out among other people. Then he would have found Catherine, and he would surely have dealt just as I did; and who knows how everything would then have fitted itself in?"

Aunt Ursul shook her large head.

"Do not sin against yourself, Lambert," said she. "I have always found that, rightly weighed, everything had to come out just as it did come out, and with this we pause."

"I, also, cannot conceive how it could have been different," replied Lambert. "As far as I can see, my hand has been little in this, and yet I might even surrender her could I thus bring Conrad back."

"And I my two hands and my head in addition," said Aunt Ursul, "could I by that means bring it about that my four boys might enter the door alive. Lambert, Lambert! let me tell you, 'if' and 'but' are very fine things, but one must keep them away from him or he will get crazy over them. I have had experience of it in myself and in my old man."

"But Conrad is not dead," said Lambert, "so all hope cannot be lost. I had also lost my head. I did not know what I said or did. He was without this already unhappy enough. Alas, aunt, I am also to blame. I would gladly tell him that. I would like to talk right into his heart. He has hitherto always been willing to listen to me. What do you advise, aunt?"

"What should I advise?" said Aunt Ursul fretfully. "It is always the old story: First you set the world on its head, and then you come running and cry: 'What do you advise, aunt?' Am I God? Many times there seems to be need of it. No, Lambert, in that you are indeed right. Conrad is not yet dead, and so we need not throw away our guns into the grain-field. But it will not do to pour out the child with the water in which you have bathed it. To pour oil into the fire increases the blaze. Should you now go to Conrad it would not be well. You can't gather ripe figs from a thorn-bush. In due time one can pick roses, Lambert, in due time."

Aunt Ursul repeated her last words several times as though she would thus help her inability to advise.

"But time is pressing," said Lambert. "Who knows how soon we shall have the French here?— Perhaps to-morrow. My God! to-morrow should be our wedding day."

He told his aunt what arrangement he had made with the minister.

"Yes, yes; man proposes, but God disposes," said Aunt Ursul. "We can now say nothing about to-morrow. This thing will probably not get so far as that by to-morrow. What concerns the other I will make my care, Lambert. Whether the maiden comes

to me, or I to her, will be about the same in the minister's eyes, to say nothing about God, who has something better to attend to than to trouble himself about
such hocus-pocus. I am here beforehand. I would
gladly have looked after my old man, who was to-
day quite desperate and heathenish, but if it must be
I too will stay. There must be some one to lead the
regiment when it comes. Still there, Pluto! What
does the beast mean? I believe the young men are
coming already. You look after them, Lambert. I
will meanwhile look after the girl; and Lambert, if
they are there, keep them before the house. The
night is warm and you can keep watch there. Whoever wishes to sleep can come in here and lie down
on the hearth, but I want him to be as still as a
mouse."

Aunt Ursul went into the room. Lambert stepped
to the front door and quieted the growling Pluto. He
listened, and now clearly heard the steps of his comrades. Soon their forms emerged out of the light fog
which had spread over the fields near the creek,
though the moon already stood at some height over
the woods. There were three of them. Lambert's
heart beat. He expected only Fritz Volz and Richard Herkimer. Was Conrad the third? Surely,
surely it must be Conrad.

But out of Pluto's broad chest sounds like rolling
thunder now broke forth. Did not the intelligent
and faithful beast know her own master? Lambert

with great eagerness went to meet those who were coming.

"God bless you, Lambert," said Richard Herkimer.

"God bless you, Lambert," said Fritz Volz.

The third one had remained a few steps behind.

"Who is the other one?" asked Lambert with trembling voice.

"Guess," said Richard laughing.

"The crazy fellow," said Fritz Volz.

"He would go with us, though Annie herself thought that he would not fire away his powder for nothing," said Richard.

"Is it Adam Bellinger?" asked Lambert.

"Now come up, you hare's foot," said Fritz Volz.

"Are you holding the dog?" asked Adam, with uncertain voice.

Richard and Fritz laughed, but Lambert could not join them, as he might have done at another time. Adam instead of Conrad! What could have moved the silly fellow to such night-wandering except the desire again to be near Catherine? What would his friends think of Catherine? What would not the talkative Adam have told them on the way.

"Come a little nearer," said Richard, having taken Lambert's arm as they were walking toward the house. "I want to say a few words to you. You must not be angry, Lambert, that we brought Adam along. He would not be set right. Heaven knows what has

come into his calf's head. We could have made
nothing out of his crazy talk, but the ladies lit the
candle so that it shone bright enough. That you—
Nay, Lambert, old boy, I wish you happiness with
all my heart. And I can also tell you that by this a
heavy stone is lifted from my heart. You know I
have always liked Annie, and she has not been un-
kind to me; but old Bellinger had got his head set
that you must become his third son-in-law—and nobody else. Now if you marry the stranger girl it will
help us all. Therefore once more, happiness and
blessing, Lambert Sternberg, with my whole heart."

"That I also wish you," said Lambert.

"I know it," said Richard; "but now we must also
say good evening to your girl, Lambert. If she is half
as handsome as Adam swears, she must be something
truly wonderful. Is she in the house?"

They stood before the door. The two others were
still some distance behind. Lambert drew his young
friend beside him on the bench and briefly told him
everything which sooner or later he would have unfolded more fully, but which now could no longer be
kept secret.

"This is my situation, Richard," concluded he.
"You can conceive how heavy my heart is."

"I can well conceive it," said Richard Herkimer,
heartily pressing Lambert's hand. "Dear friend, this
is an unhappy record. Conrad should be ashamed,
especially at this time, to forsake you and leave the

cart sticking in the mud, when even such fellows as
John Mertens and Hans Haberkorn are pulling with
us at the same rope."

"You see, Richard, it is that which grieves me most,"
said Lambert. "You know how they talked about us
last year—that we held with the French; that Conrad spoke Indian better than German, and other scan-
dalous stuff. What will they now say when they
hear that, at the very moment when the danger breaks
in upon us, Conrad is not to be found among us?"

"Let them say what they will," said Richard. "My
father, the minister, and all who are reasonably intelligent, you have always had on your side; and they
will also this time know what to think. Perhaps
Conrad also will yet consider."

"God grant it!" said Lambert, with a deep sigh.

"Now," said Richard, rising, "I will give a wink to
Fritz Volz; and then you must tell us what we are to
do for the night."

Richard Herkimer went to the two others, who
had remained standing at some distance, engaged, as
it appeared, in a discussion. At the same moment
Aunt Ursul came out of the door.

"Is that you, Lambert?"

"Yes, aunt."

"Who are the others?"

Lambert named the friends.

"What, then, does Adam want?" said Aunt Ursul.
"The fellow has become quite foolish. Nay, Lam-

bert, that is your business; but to-morrow send off
the awkward fellow.   We don't want useless eaters
here.   This evening he may come in with the rest.
Catherine is up again.   She says it is not a time now
to be sick.   In that surely she is right.   She is standing at the fire, boiling an evening soup for your people, as though nothing had happened—the noble girl!
I am now going home; and, Lambert, the minister
meant well in what he said to you, but under the circumstances it is senseless.   You are an honorable
man, and the girl is not trifling, and God knows what
your duty is in the case."

Lambert went with Aunt Ursul into the house.
Catherine came to meet him, looking pale and having
a cloth wound about her head, but greeting him with
a friendly smile.   "You must not scold me," she said.
"To please your aunt I acted as though I was asleep.
I have heard everything.   I could not remain quietly
in bed while you have so many guests.   I again feel
quite well."

She leaned her head against his breast and whispered: "And you love me notwithstanding, Lambert; not so?"

Lambert held the dear girl fast in his arms as a
loud ahem! was heard, and Aunt Ursul entered the
door closely followed by the three young men.

"So, you young people," said Aunt Ursul, "come
in and eat your supper—that is, if it is ready; and
this is my Lambert's dear bride, and she is not stand-

ing there like Lot's pillar of salt. Adam Bellinger,
you may as well shut your mouth. No roasted
pigeons will fly into it. There is for this evening a
soup, so that you must move your own hands to get
it conveniently out of the bowl. So, Richard Herkimer, that is right that you at once offer your hand
to the young lady. You are always polite, having
learned it from your father. And now I'll be off.
God protect you, Catherine, and you, Lambert, and
you all. I shall come again to-morrow and perhaps
with my old man. Now nobody needs to be farther
concerned about me. Do you hear? Aunt Ursul
can find her home alone."

While she thus spoke she took her rifle, kissed
Catherine heartily, and shook hands with the young
men one after the other. Then she walked out of
the house into the windy night.

The three guests breathed more freely when austere
Aunt Ursul had turned her broad back, and her heavy
tread outside was heard. But it was some time before they began to look about them and to talk,
though Catherine kindly invited them to take seats,
and assured them that the soup would soon be ready.

Richard Herkimer said to Fritz Volz: "Better sit
down, Fritz," though he himself remained standing.
Fritz Volz pushed Adam Bellinger in the side and
asked him if he did not see that he was standing in
the way of the young lady. Then they rubbed their
hands as if they were entirely frozen, though, at least

on Adam's brow, clear sweat drops were impearled.
And when they spoke it was in whispers, as though
the steaming soup which Catherine now placed on the
table was to be their last meal.

Adam Bellinger was not quite sure whether this
would be the case with him. Fritz Volz had before
told him that the chief business would be diligently to
patrol against the enemy, and, since he had such a
burning desire to measure himself against the French,
he must make the beginning; that it was indeed no
fun to walk about the woods in the night when there
might be a Frenchman behind every tree; but that
doubtless Adam would teach the fellows manners.
Adam said that he had come to help defend the block-
house against a possible attack, but not to let himself
be shot by the French and scalped by the Indians in
the woods in the night and fog. The contention
about this, which had before been arrested, was now
again taken up by the teasing Fritz, though with a
little timidity. He wanted to know from Adam how
he could distinguish between a tree-trunk and an Indian, in the night. Richard asked him how he would
save himself if he were suddenly seized by his long,
yellow hair from behind and jerked to the ground.
By these and other similar questions of the two teas-
ers, Adam was thrown into great distress. They
laughed loud, while he came near crying, until Catherine interposed, saying that a courageous man would
in danger hit upon the right thing, though he might

not be able to tell beforehand what he would do.

"Yes, indeed," said Adam, "the young lady has more sense in her little finger than you have in your two heads. I shall doubtless know what I have to do."

He accompanied these brave words with such a thankful, tender look at Catherine, that both the merry rogues broke out in loud laughter, and a glimmer of mirthfulness passed over Lambert's earnest face.

"It is enough," said he. "Adam will do his duty as well as the rest of us. It is time that we assign the watch for the night; two for every two hours, and Adam and I will make the beginning. Good night, Catherine."

He gave his hand to Catherine. The others followed his example. As Lambert was leaving the house Fritz Volz and Richard Herkimer came out too.

"We will also rather stay outdoors," said Richard. "Fritz, as I know by experience, cannot do without snoring and that might disturb Catherine, who surely needs sleep."

Fritz Volz said he could do without snoring, but Richard could not stop talking, and that it was on the whole better that they should camp before the door.

"You kind young men," said Lambert.

"Is that kind?" said Richard eagerly. "I would

stand all night on my head if I knew that Catherine
would sleep better on that account."

"And I would lie there in the creek up to my neck
in the water," said Fritz Volz.

Adam sighed, and looked at the moon which hung
clear and large over the forest.

"Come, Adam," said Lambert, "we will go upon
our round."

They set out, accompanied by Pluto. The others
stretched themselves out upon the dry sand before
the door, wrapped up in their blankets, their rifles
in their arms. Fritz Volz did not snore. Richard
Herkimer did not talk. Both looked up to the twinkling stars, lost in thoughts which happily remained
concealed from Gussie and Annie Bellinger.

Never before had Catherine been so carefully
guarded as during this night.

CHAPTER XII

The following day was the Sabbath, though it brought the Germans on the Mohawk and on the creek no Sabbath rest; but only labor, fatigue, alarm, distraction. From early morning it swarmed in all the settlements as in a bee-hive. Wives prepared and packed. Holes were dug in carefully selected and well-concealed places, in which such valuable things as could not well be taken along were hidden. The men got their arms in readiness, or brought the cattle from the pastures and from the woods and shut them up in the yards so that they could at any moment drive them to the fort, or to Herkimer's house, as orders had been given yesterday afternoon. Boats went busily here and there. From time to time a rider hastened to one of the rendezvous appointed for the three flying corps. A feeling of security and pride took possession of all when such a squadron, consisting of twenty-four well mounted and armed young men, under the lead of Charles Herkimer, Richard's oldest brother, trotted up the river toward Black River to reconnoiter. By noon the two new ferries were also ready. All felt assured of the usefulness of these arrangements, now that it had come to the point of actual flight, though yesterday they had met with earnest opposition. However, more than one could hardly believe in such a possibility, for the sun in the blue sky shone down so golden, the birds sang so blithely in the trees, and over the fields from the little church on the hill came the clear sound of the small bell. But, indeed, on the twelfth of November of the year before, the sun also rose clear, and when it had gone down its last rays had fallen on the ruins of more than one burned house, and more than one was lying in the fields who would never again see it rise. The remembrance of that dreadful day was yet too fresh to allow the thoughtless to shut out the seriousness of the situation; and the bitter thought that they would have to answer for leaving house and home unprotected from the ruthless enemy, reminded them of Herkimer's words the day before, that everything, except life itself, can again be arranged, and can be more or less easily made to accommodate itself to the inevitable.

Also in the otherwise so quiet house on the creek there was to-day a restless urgency. Jacob Ehrlich and Anthony Bierman had come from the Mohawk, accoutered with their rifles and a large sack of ammunition, which Herkimer had given them, and which the stout young men had carried by turns the whole distance up the creek. Now the powder, to which each added his own store, was equally divided, and the caliber of the rifles was measured, whence it appeared that two different sizes of bullets must be cast.

With this Lambert intrusted Adam Bellinger, after,
under four eyes, not without a certain solemnity, he
had said that it was his earnest desire to stay and
take part in every danger with him and the rest. He
knew about the French, but would rather hear the
whistling of their bullets and the Indian's war-whoop
than the laughter of the women at home should he
now return without having accomplished anything.
Lambert pitied the poor fellow, and the ,more since
Catherine took kindly to her foolish admirer and
laughed in a friendly way at his peculiarities.

In the council of war held by the young men it was
decided that they must leave the door-yard, which
for good reasons had been made to extend a considerable distance from the house, as it was, and that
their defense must be confined to the house itself.
The proposition of Richard to conduct the water of
the creek into the dry ditch which encircled the foot
of the hill outside of the stone inclosure was discarded
as evidently requiring too much time. Instead of
this it was decided to deepen the partly filled ditch as
much as they could, and in many places where the
wall was broken down to repair and raise it and entirely to block up the passage-way through it opposite
the house-door with stones and plank, and meanwhile
use a bridge over the wall and dug-way that could be
easily removed. There was found little to do to the
house itself, though they looked carefully after the
strong shutters with which the port-holes of the

ground-floor, like those of a war-ship, could be closed from within, and so also at those covering the round holes in the gallery, through which they could fire at an enemy from above, should he be able to reach the house and come beneath the gallery. In the roof were cut several trap-doors, so that here also those approaching could be greeted with two very long-range rifles.

While the men were thus engaged, Catherine and Aunt Ursul, who had again come early in the morning, did not remain unemployed. Fortunately water did not first have to be brought. The spring carried into the house by the intelligent and indescribable labor of Lambert's father, furnished plentifully all that was needed. But for the moment the supply of provisions seemed to be inadequate. During Lambert's absence Conrad had lived from hand to mouth, according to his hunter's custom, and Catherine had manifestly had no time to supply what was lacking. So Adam had repeatedly to go empty to the Ditmar house, which happily was not far, and come back loaded with loaves of bread, hams and other good things—every time received with a loud hallo by his merry companions—until Aunt Ursul declared that there was enough to last eight days. For still better provision a couple of wethers of Lambert's small flock were driven into the inclosure where also Hans was pastured on the short grass, and often shook his thick head and looked at Lambert with his intelligent eyes, as though he wished to know what the unusual rush to-day might mean, and whether he must walk about saddled all day. But it might be that at any moment a message had to be sent, and Hans had to be ready.

So they labored busily in the work of fortifying, and were toward noon engaged in erecting the fire-signal, when a rider on a gray horse became visible, as he was coming up the valley on a trot.

"Herkimer! Herkimer!" called out Fritz Volz, who first saw him.

"Yes, it is father," said Richard in confirmation.

A few minutes later the distinguished man stopped before the door, and was respectfully greeted by Lambert and the other young men.

"I have no time to stop," said Herkimer, "and only wanted to see how far you have got. Now this looks well. Could you fill the ditch with water it would indeed be better; but this would be a long and wearisome labor, and you will have to dispense with it. How are you off for ammunition? Do you think you have enough, Lambert?"

Herkimer had now dismounted, and he asked Lambert and Aunt Ursul, who had meanwhile come out of the house, to give him detailed account of the condition of things, by means of which he knew how to bring it about that they should get some distance from the others.

He then said, "I would like to speak to you alone.

I feel sure of you, and of Richard, but I am not so
certain of the others, whom I do not know so well.
You will here, so far as one can now judge, have a
difficult position.   I this morning received intelli-
gence that the French have at least three hundred
men, and that besides this the Onondagas and the
Oneidas will join them.   The bargain is indeed not
yet concluded, but will doubtless be made if our last
means fail—I mean if Conrad is not in a position to
bring his old friends into a different state of mind.   I
have from the governor the long-expected authority
to yield to them everything possible, and can intrust
Conrad with it.   He or nobody is in a situation to
turn away from us this great misfortune.   Where is
he?   I have not yet seen him."

"Hurry over there, Lambert.   Those sparrow-heads
will not finish without you," said Aunt Ursul.

The poor boy!" she proceeded, as Lambert went
away with red cheeks and a thankful look at Aunt
Ursul, "the poor, dear boy! his heart is being eaten
out; and that so that now the whole world must become acquainted with his brother's shame, which is
really his own shame.   Nay, you are indeed not sponsor for the whole world, Herkimer, but in this case
you must be satisfied with me."

She then briefly told Herkimer all that it was necessary for him to know.

The excellent man listened with an earnest,
thoughtful mien, and there lay a deep pain in the

tone of his voice as now, shaking his gray head, he said:

"So we Germans will not unitedly resist our natural enemy. That Conrad should now fail us is a sad misfortune. His quarrel with Lambert at this moment means, not one friend less, but several hundred enemies more. Yes, why do I say hundred? The example of the Oneidas may become the measure of all the nations along the lakes, and then our well-being—our peace—is past for a long time, perhaps forever!"

Nicolas Herkimer sighed, and struck his forehead with his hand.

"Now," said he, "what one cannot hinder one must let happen, and, in any case, poor Catherine cannot help it. Let us go in a few moments, aunt, I would like to form the acquaintance of the maiden who so turns the heads of our young men."

Catherine, who was busily engaged at the hearth in her preparations for dinner, had paid no attention to what was going on outside. She had just stepped to the door to look for Aunt Ursul, and suddenly saw a strange and very stately man opposite to her, in whom she at once recognized Nicolas Herkimer. A deep blush flew over her cheeks; then, however, she approached without being confused, and put her hand in Herkimer's offered right hand.

"Poor child!" said he, holding her thin fingers for a moment, "the life that awaits you here is very rough.   May the strength you need not be wanting to you."

"Ah, what, sponsor," said Aunt Ursul; "do not make the maiden shy.   You think because she has hands like a princess—but it depends not on the hands, but on the heart, sponsor—and that I assure you is in the right place.   So much I can tell you."

"Should you not say it, those eyes would do so," said Herkimer smiling—"at least to me, who am old enough to look into them without being punished for it.   Now, my dear girl, you need not blush.   You see my hair is getting gray, so a joke may be allowed. Live happy, Aunt Ursul.   Live happy, kind maiden; and may heaven grant that we may joyfully meet again."

He said the last words also to the young men, who had finished their work and had come up.   Then he pressed the hand of each one in turn, holding that of his son Richard perhaps a moment longer, swung himself on the gray, and rode off on a sharp trot without looking back.

"That is an Israelite indeed, in whom there is no guile," said Aunt Ursul.   "And now, children, let us go to the table.   I have an appetite like a wild wolf."

Notwithstanding this information, at the dinner to which they now sat down Aunt Ursul ate almost nothing, and also, contrary to her custom, was very still.   Toward the last she took no part whatever in the conversation, and first woke from her absentmindedness when Anthony Bierman, who had the watch, announced the minister.

"Who?" called Aunt Ursul, as she quickly rose from her chair; "the minister? He comes at the right time for me. God has sent him. Keep your seats; do you hear?"

Aunt Ursul hastily left the house and went to meet the minister, who, with rapid strides, was approaching, having his hat, wig and snuff-box in one hand, and in the other a colored pocket handkerchief with which he was wiping his bald head.

"I know it already," he called out, as soon as he caught sight of Aunt Ursul. "Herkimer, who met me between your house and Volz', has told me everything."

"So much the better," replied Aunt Ursul, "and now, dominie, don't talk as loud as if you were standing in the pulpit. The young folks are within, and must not hear what we are doing here. Come close."

She led the minister away from the house to the wall of the door-yard, where nobody could hear except Hans, who now raised his thick head and with a bit of grass in his mouth observantly looked at the two with his black eyes from under his bushy foretop.

"What business have you to listen? Go your way," said Aunt Ursul to the horse.

"But, Aunt Ursul, what in all the world is it all about?" asked the minister.

"You shall soon hear," replied Aunt Ursul, whose

glances wandered from the edge of the woods to the sky, and from there again toward the woods, and at last, with a peculiar expression of face, rested on the minister.

"You are nòt married, dominie, and for what you do, or leave undone, you are accountable to nobody."

"What do you mean by that?" asked the minister.

"My old man is seventy-one, and I do not believe that he will last much longer," remarked Ursul thoughtfully.

The minister held the pinch of snuff, that he had meant to apply to his nose, between his fingers, and looked attentively at Aunt Ursul.

"Should he live longer, he has had me thirty years; and sometime everything must come to an end; so we are very properly called and chosen thereto."

The minister dropped the pinch of snuff. "For God's sake, Aunt Ursul, what are you driving at?"

"I took you to be more courageous," said Aunt Ursul.

"And I you to be more rational," said the minister.

"About such things one must ask his own heart," said Aunt Ursul.

"And the heart is a timorous, perverse thing," replied the minister.

"Yes, very timid," said Aunt Ursul, scornfully.

"Yes; truly perverse," said the minister guardedly.

"Now, without further parley, will you be my man, or not?" said Aunt Ursul who had lost patience.

"God forbid!" said the minister, who could no longer control his repugnance.

"Indeed, you look like a man," said Aunt Ursul contemptuously, turning on her heel.

"Are you then entirely God-forsaken, unhappy woman?" said the minister, laying his fleshy hand on Aunt Ursul's shoulder.

"Not I, but you, hare-hearted man," said Aunt Ursul, shaking off his hand and turning, vigorously away. "You who always preach about sacrifice and love, and have neither the one nor the other; and shear the cuckoo for the lost lamb, if you can only sit quietly by your flesh-pots. Now then stay, in the devil's name—God forgive me the sin—I shall be able alone to find the road to my poor, misguided boy, and God will give me the right words to touch his heart."

Again Aunt Ursul turned away. The minister slapped his forehead, and with a few rapid steps overtook her as she was hastening from him.

"Aunt Ursul!"

"What do you want?"

"Naturally I will go with you."

"For once."

"For once and every time. By the thousand, woman! why did you not tell me at once that it was something about Conrad?"

"About whom else should it be?"

"About many things. Forget what I have said.

I give you my word as a man and as a servant of
God that it was a misunderstanding—of which I am
ashamed—and for which I ask your pardon. When
shall we start?"

Aunt Ursul shook her head. She could not conceive what her old friend had before thought, but she
felt that he was now fully resolved, and minutes were
precious.

"At once naturally," she replied to his last question.

"I am ready."

"So! Come in and say a friendly word to the girl,
and let nothing be noticed. Lambert must not know
what we have in hand. Nobody must know. If we
succeed in bringing him back it is well; if not, let his
shame be buried with us. In either case they must
not feel concerned about us. It is possible, dominie,
that we shall never return. You comprehend that
clearly?"

"God's will be done," said the minister.

CHAPTER XIII

Two hours later, Aunt Ursul and the minister were already deep in the forest, away from the creek, on a narrow Indian path, which was as well the path of the buffalo and the deer. But Pluto, going before the wanderers, with her broad nose near the ground and her long, restless tail wagging, did not follow the tracks of buffalo or deer. More than once she turned away from a fresh track into the woods, every time soon to return into the path.

"You see now, dominie, how well it is that I went back to fetch the dog on an occasion like this," said Aunt Ursul. "You were impatient at the losing of time, but we are well paid for it."

"It was not on account of the delay," replied the minister. "I was afraid that, in spite of our large circuit, they would guess our purpose. Both Lambert and Catherine looked at us with an expression which, as I read it, meant: 'We know what you are up to!'"

"They know nothing," said Aunt Ursul. "Why should I not call out the dog for my own and my old man's greater security?"

"Because nobody would really believe that you are so disturbed by fear."

"Well," said Aunt Ursul, "let them think what

182

they please.   Without the dog we should fail, and so
let us push on."

"I am not quite sure that we shall so reach our
end, Aunt Ursul."

"Are you already tired?"

"I tire not so easily, in such an affair, you know.
But who can assure us that Conrad, in his anger and
despondency, has not walked as far as his feet would
carry him, which at last must be farther than we with
our best will can go.   And there is another possibility, of which I think with trembling."

"That my young man has gone over to them?"
cried Aunt Ursul, turning so quickly that the minister, who was close behind, jumped back a step.   "Do
you mean that?"

"God forbid!" replied the minister, displeased at
Aunt Ursul's question, and that by its earnestness his
opened snuff-box was almost knocked out of his hand.
"But he who lays his hand upon his brother, as Conrad has done, may also lay his hand upon himself.   As
far as I know Conrad, the last will be at least as easy
as the first."

"You, however, do not know my young man,"
said Aunt Ursul earnestly, and she went on in more
quiet tones: "See, dominie, I admit that the young
man, at this moment, does not value his life more
than a pine cone, but, notwithstanding, I would swear
that he will sell it dear.   And who shall pay for it?
The French and their base Indians.   That you may

depend on. And see, dominie, that is also the reason why I am thoroughly convinced that he has not
gone as far as his feet could carry him, but is some-
where here near by, and is keeping sharp watch over
the house in which his parents lived, whose door-sill
he will never again cross. He may keep his word,
but be assured, dominie, if the enemy get so far they
will have to come over his dead body."

Deeply moved, Aunt Ursul was silent. The minister, though not entirely convinced, thought it prudent not to express his opinion.

So they went on for some time in silence. The
dog ran ahead, or out to one or the other side of the
path, at one moment stopping and smelling up in the
air, then again eagerly following a track. Aunt
Ursul's sharp, knowing eyes watched every movement of the animal, and often she gently said:
"Search, Pluto!—that is right, Pluto," more to herself than to the dog, for she needed little encourage-
ment. The minister kept his eyes fixed on Aunt
Ursul's broad back, and conversed with her when the
path did not require all his attention.

This indeed was often the case, and soon the path
became so difficult for their unaccustomed feet that
conversation stopped entirely. Ever rougher and
steeper became the ascent over the great roots of the
old forest pines. Ever more wildly roared the creek
among the sharp rocks, until at length in a deep cleft
under overhanging vines it entirely disappeared from

the wanderers. Following the dog, they now turned
off to the right into the woods, and, laboriously going
up a few hundred steps, reached the top of the plateau.

Here the minister, whose strength was nearly exhausted, would gladly have rested a few moments;
but Aunt Ursul, with an expressive look, pointed to
the dog, which with great jumps, as though full of
joy, ran about a pine which stretched up giant-like in
the midst of a little opening.

"There he lay," said Aunt Ursul, almost breathless from excitement and joy. "Here, in this spot,
he lay. Do you see, dominie, the impression in the
moss and the crushed bushes? There also is a torn
piece of paper. Here he put a new load in his rifle.
Further, dominie, further. I would swear that in
less than half an hour we will have himself. Further!
Further!"

The energetic woman shoved her rifle, which had
slid off by her bending over, more securely on her
shoulder, and took several long steps, as the dog,
which for a moment had stood motionless with raised
head looking into the woods, suddenly, with a loud
bark and breaking through the bushes with great
leaps, disappeared in the forest.

"Now, God help us! what then has the beast?"
said the minister, coming up panting.

"Her master," replied Aunt Ursul. "Still!"

Bending her body she stared with great round eyes

at the thicket in which the dog had disappeared. The minister's heart throbbed ready to burst. He would gladly have taken a pinch of snuff, as he usually did when peculiarly excited, but Aunt Ursul had laid her hand on his arm, and her brown fingers pressed harder and harder.

Still!" said she again, though the minister neither spoke nor stirred. ' Don't you hear anything?"

"No," said the minister.

"But I do."

A peculiar sound, half a call, half a sob, came from her throat. She let go the arm of the minister and hastened in the same direction the dog had taken. But she had not yet reached the edge of the opening, when the bushes separated and Conrad stepped out, accompanied by Pluto, barking with joy and jumping up against her master. Aunt Ursul could not or would not check her walk. She threw herself forward on Conrad's breast, who with strong arms embraced the good aunt, his second mother, bending his face over her shoulder to conceal the tears streaming from his eyes.

So the two stood, encircled in each other's arms, and the light of the evening sun played so beautifully about the handsome picture that the eyelashes of the minister became moist.

He stepped up gently, and, laying one hand on Conrad's shoulder and the other on that of his aunt, said heartily: "Here my blessing is not needed, but I must be permitted to rejoice with you."

"God bless you, dominie!" said Conrad, raising himself up and reaching out his hand to the worthy man. "This is handsome in you that you have accompanied aunt. I did not expect you, at least not both of you."

"Yet, Conrad," said Aunt Ursul, interrupting him, "why are you ashamed to tell the truth? You did expect me!"

"Well, yes," said Conrad.

"And I have brought him along," Aunt Ursul added, "because you know him from childhood, that he is a good and righteous man; and in such a case a man can speak better to a man than a poor woman like me, for the cuckoo knows how it looks in your hard hearts."

Conrad's handsome countenance darkened while his aunt spoke in this manner. His eyes looked angry from under his sunken eyelashes. However, he forced himself to speak with apparent calmness, saying: "I thank you again; but, aunt, and you, dominie, I beg you say nothing about him—you know whom I mean —and also nothing about her. I can't hear it and I won't hear it. It may be that I am wrong, but I have taken my stand and will take the consequences."

"Now," said Aunt Ursul to the minister, "you must open your mouth. For what else did I bring you along?"

Aunt Ursul was quite angry. She felt a secret sympathy with Conrad, and had at the same time an obscure feeling that, in his condition, she would think and speak and act in the same manner. She could say nothing more, in a case in which her heart sided so painfully with the one who was in the wrong.

The minister, in his excitement, took one pinch of snuff after the other. Then he sought unavailingly for the few remaining particles, closed his box, put it in his pocket, and said: "Conrad, listen quietly to me a few minutes. I think I can tell you something of which you have, perhaps, not so earnestly thought. Whether you are wrong in regard to your brother and the maiden—whom I to-day first learned to know, and who appears to be a good, brave girl—or not, I will not decide, nor will I examine into the matter. I have never been married, nor, so far as I know, in love, but once, and that so long ago that it may well be that I do not understand such things. But, Conrad, there are brothers whom we cannot renounce. There are father's houses which must be sacred to us under all circumstances. In the one case we are of the same lineage; in the other it is our home-land. On this account, to us driven away and thrust out— to us pressed down and shaken together by strangers in a strange land—must those relatives who are still left—must the country of our new home, be twice and thrice holy. And there is nothing, Conrad, that can release us from this duty; no strife with a brother, no wish to have a wife, no rights as to mine and thine, for here there is no mine and thine, but only *our*, as

in the prayer we offer to God in whom we all believe.
I know well, Conrad, that this feeling of holy duty
has not died out of your heart; that, on the other hand,
you will in your own way satisfy it. But, Conrad,
your way is not a good one, even were you determined, as we all suppose, to sacrifice your life.   I
tell you, Conrad, God will not accept the offering.
He will reject it, as he did Cain's sacrifice, and your
precious blood will run down into the sand useless
and unhonored."

The minister's deep voice had an unusually solemn
tone, in this forest stillness; and as he now, on account of his emotion, which beautifully illuminated
his plain face, was silent a few moments, it roared
through the branches of the giant pines as if God
himself and not a man had spoken.

So at least it seemed to good Aunt Ursul, and the
same feeling was able also to touch the wild and perverse heart of Conrad. His broad breast rose and fell
powerfully; his face had a peculiar, constrained expression; his eyes were fixed on the ground, and his
strong hands, which grasped the barrel of his gun,
trembled.

The minister began anew: "Your precious blood
—I say, Conrad, precious, as all human blood is
precious, but doubly precious in the hour of danger,
thrice precious when it flows in the veins of a man to
whom the God of all has given the power to be the
protection and defense of those nearest to him. More-

over, Conrad, to whom much is given, of him shall
much be required. The rest of us are only like
soldiers in rank and file, and we need not be ashamed
of it. But you are looked upon as holding a more
important position, and I need only to mention it so
that you may return to yourself. You will not shrink
from a task that you and you only of us all are fitted
for. Nicolas Herkimer has learned that negotiations
are taking place between our enemies and the Oneidas; that they are only delaying their attack until a
treaty is concluded, in order that then they may fall
upon us with resistless power. You know that our
holding of the Oneidas will secure to us the other nations on the lakes. You know that thus far they
have been a wall to us behind which we felt measura-
bly secure. You have lived for years with the Oneidas. You speak their language; you are highly re-
spected by them; you know the way to their hearts.
Now then, Conrad, it is the wish and will of Herkimer, our captain, that you go at once to them, and
in his name, and in that of the governor, assure them
of the yielding of all points lately in controversy between them and the government to their satisfaction,
and according to their own views, if they will abide by
the old protection and alliance which they entered
into with us—yes, if they only will not take part
against us in the present war. You notice and understand the proposition, so that I, a man little accustomed to such things, need not go into particulars.

I now ask you, Conrad Sternberg, will you, as is your bounden duty, carry out the orders of our captain?"

"It is too late," said Conrad, with broken voice.

"Why too late?"

"What you fear has already taken place. The Oneidas have joined the French and the Onondagas. This morning—yes, an hour ago—I could yet have gone to them unobserved to bring about what you propose. Now it is impossible."

"How do you know it, Conrad?" asked the minister and Aunt Ursul, as if out of the same mouth.

"Come," said Conrad.

He hung his rifle over his shoulder, and now walked before them both diagonally through the forest, which was constantly becoming lighter until the ·tall trees stood singly among the low bushes. Here he moved carefully in a bent posture and indicated to the two by signs that they should follow his example. At last he fell on his knees, bent a couple of bushes slowly apart, and winked to the others to come up in the same way. They did so, and looked through the opening, as through a little window for observation in a door, on an unusual spectacle.

Beneath them, at the foot of the steep mass of rocks on the edge of which they were, there spread out a broad, meadow-like valley, which on the opposite side was encircled by precipitous, wood-covered rocks, and through it in many windings a creek gently ran. On the bank of the creek next to them there

was a space covered with small, canvas-walled tents
and lodges, standing without order. Between the
tents and lodges there burned a couple of dozen fires
whose rising smoke, glowing in the evening sun,
spread out above in a dark cloud, through which the
scene below looked more phantasmal. There was a
mass of people in active movement—French, some
regulars and some volunteers, many without any dis-
tinctive mark—and, in greater number, Indians, whose
half-naked bodies, adorned with variously colored
war-paint, shone in the light of the sun. The groups
on the bank of the creek stood close together, and it
was not difficult to discover the reason. On the other
side, the band of Indians there gathered must have
arrived recently. Some were engaged in putting up
their wigwams, others were kindling fires. The most
of them, however, stood at the edge of the creek talking with those on the other side. The creek, of mod-
erate breadth, had washed out for itself a deep bed in
the meadow-land, with steep sides. They could not
well come together without bridges, and these were
hastily made for the occasion with tree-trunks, while
here and there the willful or eager swam across, or,
trying to jump across and in most cases falling short,
occasioned every time shouts of laughter among those
looking on.

With beating hearts Aunt Ursul and the minister in
succession observed the spectacle which had to them
such a terrible meaning. Then following Conrad's

whispered request, they withdrew as carefully as they had crept up, back through the bushes into the woods.

"How many are there?" asked Aunt Ursul.

"Four hundred besides the Oneidas," replied Conrad. "The Oneidas are quite as strong, if they allow all their warriors to be called into the field. I have just counted two hundred and fifty. Anyhow, the others will follow, otherwise they would find no preparations for the night."

"But will they go on at once?" asked Aunt Ursul.

"Certainly, for they know that the hours are precious. So you will doubtless by to-morrow noon have them on your necks."

"*You?*" said the minister impressively. "You should say '*We*,' Conrad."

Conrad did not answer, but went silently and without turning into the border of the woods far enough from the edge of the plateau to prevent their being seen. After going about two hundred steps they came to a place where there was a deep ravine, which led from the heights above by a sort of natural rock-stairs into the valley. Above, where the stairs opened on the plateau, there was a narrow, deep-cut path entirely blocked by a cunningly devised obstruction of tree-trunks, stones and brush. Other stones, some of them very large, were pushed so close to the sides of the ditch that with a lever, or perhaps even with the foot, they could be slid off on those coming up the path. It looked as if a dozen strong men must have labored for days to perform such a work. Conrad's giant strength accomplished it in a few hours.

"Here," said he, turning to his companions with his peculiar laugh, "here I intended to wait until the last stone had been thrown off and my last cartridge had been shot."

"And then?" asked Aunt Ursul.

"Break in two my rifle on the head of the first one that should come up into the narrow path."

"And now?" asked the minister, seizing the hand of the wild man; "and now, Conrad?"

"Now I will carry out the orders of Herkimer."

"For God's sake!" cried Aunt Ursul. "It would clearly be your destruction; the Onondagas, your enemies, would pull you to pieces!"

"Hardly," replied Conrad. "The Oneidas would not consent to it—at least without quarreling and strife. By this means already much would be gained, and thus I would keep them back longer than if I opposed them here, where I would in a few hours be killed. But I hope it will come out better. I would already have gone over to the Oneidas this morning, when they lay in the woods, but I had nothing to offer them. Now this is different. Perhaps I may be able to talk them over. At least I will try. Goodbye, both of you."

He reached out his hands to them. Aunt Ursul threw herself into his arms as though she would not again let her beloved young man be separated from her; but Conrad, with gentle force, freed himself and said:

"There is not a minute to be lost. I must make a wide circuit in order to come from the other side into the valley, and you have a long journey. The dog I shall take along. She can be of no use to you on the way home. Can you find the way without her, aunt? Now then good-bye; good-bye all!"

"In the hope of again seeing you," said the minister.

Conrad's face was convulsed for a moment. "As God will," he answered, in subdued tones.

The next minute they two were alone. For a moment they heard his retreating steps. Then all was still.

"We shall not see him again," said Aunt Ursul.

"We *shall* see him again," said the minister, looking at the purple clouds shining through the branches. "God helps the courageous."

"Then he will help him," said Aunt Ursul. "A more courageous heart than that of my young man beats in no human breast. God be gracious to him!"

"Amen!" said the minister.

They turned back on their homeward journey, back through the primitive forest, over which now the evening shadows were fast gathering.

CHAPTER XIV

The minister had not deceived himself when, at their departure from the block-house, he thought he read in Lambert's and Catherine's manner that they both perceived what he and Aunt Ursul contemplated, in spite of all their precautions. Indeed, while Lambert was guiding the labor of fortifying, and was himself taking an active hand in the work, his mind was constantly oppressed with heavy cares about Conrad. His heart, full of love, and needing love, could not bear the thought that his brother should be so unhappy while he was so happy—that for the first time he could not give the best part of the sunshine of life to him for whom hitherto no sacrifice had been too heavy. No, not him could he give—but he would give—not for all the world—not for his soul's salvation. Here there was no doubt—there *could be* no doubt—for this would have been the basest treachery toward himself, and toward the dear girl who had trustfully given him her pure maiden heart. And yet —and yet—

Catherine's heart was scarcely less sad. She held Lambert so unspeakably dear, and her first experience must be that she was bringing to her beloved great suffering as her first gift. She saw, indeed, no

mark of sorrow in the countenance of the precious
man. She had learned too well to read those smooth
and honorable lines. There was no dark cloud on
that open brow, no gloomy falling of those mild, blue
eyes, no sad contortion about the mouth, which otherwise so readily and often opened in friendly smiles,
but which was now closed so fast.

Thus they, without needing to speak about winning
back Conrad, had thought and brooded; and when
Aunt Ursul, yesterday, brought in the minister, and
scarcely left the good man time to sit down and eat
his dinner, but soon drove him up again and with
him left the block-house, and a few minutes after returned and called Pluto out, as though she no longer
placed any reliance on Melac, her watch-dog at home,
Lambert and Catherine gave each other an expressive look, and as soon as they were alone fell into
each other's arms and said:

"Perhaps, perhaps everything will come out right
yet."

However sad the minds of the lovers, they kept
their sadness to themselves; and the rest were little
inclined to trouble themselves about an anxiety which
was so carefully concealed from them; though Richard Herkimer, Lambert remembered, had said it was
a pity that Conrad should just at this time show his
folly. The others had spoken in a similar manner,
but with that on their part the matter was laid aside.
With or without Conrad, they were determined to

do their duty; and this certainty raised the spirits of the brave young men to unwonted courage. One added circumstance gave a peculiar impulse to this courageous feeling and enabled them to look upon the very important position in which they found themselves in an entirely poetic light. The excellent young men were all quite enchanted with Catherine's beauty and loveliness, and gave to this enchantment the most harmless and delightful expression. If Catherine at the table said a friendly word, there shone five pairs of white rows of teeth. If she expressed a wish, or only indicated one with her eyes, ten hands were stretched out—ten legs began to move. Wherever she went or stood, she had two or three attentive listeners at her side who watched with the greatest eagerness and sought to anticipate her wishes. It was a conviction firmly fixed in the mind of each that for Catherine's sake they were willing not only to be killed, but to die in the most barbaric manner the cruel nature of the Indian had discovered. So, on one occasion, when Lambert was not present, in an overflow of heroism, on Richard Herkimer's special suggestion, they all five had agreed and had shaken hands on it and promised that, whichever of them should outlive the rest, before he died himself he would kill Catherine, so that she should not fall into the enemy's hands.

This agreement of tragic sacrifice did not in any way hinder the five heroes from trying their wit on each other, and, together with their sympathy for the beautiful maiden, to tease and joke each other in every way. Poor Adam had to suffer the most from this habit. They tried to convince the good young man that Lambert had laid away a bullet which was not intended for the French, and that they were not surprised that Lambert should think no one dangerous to him besides Adam. Fritz Volz and Richard Herkimer—that he well knew himself—had already made their selection. Jacob Ehrlich and Anton Bierman were secretly weeping for their treasures that they had left on the Mohawk. Adam had already for years been going about like a roaring lion seeking whom he might devour; that he was a wandering terror and a constant care for all bridegrooms and unmarried young men; that the others had been commanded to come, but that Adam came of his own accord; and that he should tell them to what end and for what purpose, as he stood guard last evening, he had sung so sweetly: "How beautiful shines on us the morning star," that Catherine had cried and said: "Now listen to Adam, who sings sweeter than a nightingale."

Adam did not fail to reply to his tormentors. They should only concern themselves about their own affairs; that he knew what he was about. Then again, in a weeping tone, he would beg and beseech the friends to tell him truly whether Lambert had indeed formed such a shameful purpose, and whether

Catherine had really found and declared his singing so fine, and that in this life she only wanted one thing and that was a blonde lock from the head of the singer to take with her into the grave. The friends swore high and low that each of them had heard it out of Catherine's own mouth, and that each of them had promised to fulfill her special wish, and that Adam should now freely give up his scalp-lock before the Indians took it by force and the skin with it. Adam resisted, and called for help until the surrounding space resounded with shouts and laughter.

It was in the afternoon when Lambert, driven from the house by unrest, walked slowly along the bank of the creek up toward the woods. He stopped a moment and shook his head as the noise from the house struck his ear, and then again went on. They could joke and laugh, those good comrades, in this hour of sorrow and need, which oppressed his soul with leaden weight. And yet they well knew that this hour might be their last. They also had parents at home and sisters, and one and another had a girl whom he loved, and the life of these people also hung on the cast of a die. But then, they were all much younger than he, and took life so much lighter—as light as one must take it at last and be done with it so as not to sink under the burden. Was he not already too old to load more on himself—he, to whom the old burden was already so heavy to carry? How often had the rest jeered him on this account; called

him Hans the dreamer; using as a by-word when anything more serious occurred: "For this let God and
Lambert Sternberg provide." Yes, indeed, he had
learned to know care early enough, when his mother
died leaving him alone with his peevish, passionate
father; and he had to play the mediator between him
and the wild Conrad, and their relatives and the rest.
And then, after his father's death, all the labor for
the common good fell upon him, if there was any
failure on the part of the neighbors. So he had always labored and cared, and had well understood this
spring that he must undertake the difficult and responsible mission to New York. He had undertaken
it, as he did everything which was too burdensome
for others, without thinking of pay, without expect-
ing the thanks of those who had given him their commission   Now heaven had so arranged that he should
find her from whom one look, one word was pay and
thanks for all that he had done—for all that he had
suffered. The pay was too great, the thanks were
too much. He had perceived this from the beginning. Who could honorably begrudge him his unex-
pected happiness, obtained after fearful misgivings?
Not the neighbors, who would hardly forgive him for
preferring a stranger to their daughters. Not Aunt
Ursul, who, though her honest and righteous disposition strove against it, yet would rather see Conrad
in his place. And Conrad himself—his only, his beloved brother—yes, that was the deepest grief; that

was the drop bitter as gall, poured into the sweet
draught of love, and which he must always taste.   It
ought not to be so.   If this should not be so what
purpose, what meaning had the rest?   Why care for
a future that could no more bring him true joy?
Why cling to a life that had become so burdensome
to him?   Why undertake the heavy conflict that was
imminent?   Why hope to come out of this battle as
victor?   There the grass was growing in his fields.
Must it be trampled?   There his cattle were, wandering in the wilderness.   Must they fall as booty into the
hands of the enemy?   There stood his barn.   Must
it go up in flames?   There was his strongly built
house.   Must he and she be buried beneath its fragments?

Thus, in deep, oppressive anxiety, Lambert stood
at the edge of the forest, looking over the valley that
contained his home, glittering in the bright sunlight.
There was no noise in the wide circuit except the
buzz of insects over the soft bending grass and flowers of the prairie, and an occasional bird-note from
the branches of the dark-green pines which, motionless, drank in the heat of the sun.   Was then everything which had passed through his brain a heavy,
fearful dream, out of which he could wake when he
pleased?   Was the signal pile there, which with its
smoke and fire should warn the rest down the creek,
erected for a joke?   Did Aunt Ursul, who, full of
care, had the evening before sent Fritz Volz at a late

hour to tell them that she had certain knowledge that the enemy was quite near, and that they should keep the sharpest watch—did Aunt Ursul only imagine that it was so?

There! What sound was that which that instant struck his sharp ear out of the woods? There was a cracking and crushing in the dry branches, as when a deer runs with full speed through the bushes. No, it is not a deer. He now clearly heard another sound which could only be produced by the foot of a man running for his life. Nearer and nearer, down the creek, down the steep, stony, bushy path, in mad leaps, as when a stone is pushed down over a slope, came the runner.

A sudden, joyful fear rushed through Lambert's soul. In all the world but one foot could step like that—his brother's foot. In breathless, intense emotion he stands there, his wildly beating heart almost leaping from his breast. He wishes to call, but the sound sticks in his throat. He tries to run to meet him, but his knees tremble under him. At the next moment Conrad, breaking through the bushes, is at his side, and his faithful dog with mighty leaps comes with him.

"Conrad!" cried Lambert, "Conrad!"

He rushed to his brother and encircled him in his arms. All that had just now troubled him so dreadfully is forgotten. Now come what will, it is worth while to live, and also, if it must be, to die.

"Are they coming, Conrad?"

"In one hour they will be here!"

CHAPTER XV

The certainty that now the decisive moment had come, and the joy that the same moment had brought back his brother, again gave Lambert a touch of the peculiarities on account of which young and old valued and praised him—calmness, circumspection, confidence. Without hesitating a moment as to what was next to be done, and calling to his brother to notify those in the house, he hastened across the plank over the creek to the hill yonder, where the signal pile had been erected, which from there could be clearly seen from Ditmar's house away from the creek. A minute later there rose from the lofty, ingeniously constructed wood-pile a dark column of smoke, pushing its way up like the stem of a mighty palm, and spreading out above in the still air like an immense crown. Then, a quarter of a mile down the creek, there came up a dark cloud of smoke. Uncle Ditmar has kept good watch. The signal has been answered and carried farther. In a quarter of an hour they will also know on the Mohawk, six miles farther, that here on the creek the enemy has broken in. Then back over the creek—a strong push—the fastening is broken off. The plank floats away.

"Are you here yet, Conrad? How the rest will rejoice! Come!"

Lambert hastened ahead. Conrad followed with
slow, lingering steps. Was it fatigue after the dreadful running? Had the blood with which his leathern
jacket was dotted spurted from his veins?

So asked Lambert, but received no answer. And
now they had reached the temporary bridge, where
the friends who stood on the wall received them with
loud cheers. Lambert hastened up and shook the hand
of each brave youth with heartfelt joy. Conrad still
lingered at the foot of the bridge. His face was pale,
and as if emaciated with bodily pain, or an inward
conflict. He had sworn with a terrible oath that
he would not again cross the door-sill of his father's
house, or his blood should pay the forfeit. The
strong, wild heart shrunk together in his breast. His
blood—why should this trouble him? He had not
spared it. He had, a quarter of an hour ago in a battle which he alone could take up—which he alone
could bring to a happy issue—put it at hazard. But
his word! his word! that he had never yet broken—
which he now shall break—*must* break, as his clearer
soul tells him—as his noble heart bids him, in spite
of all.

As he still lingered, Catherine was suddenly standing among his cheering companions. On her account
had he renounced his father's house. As if blinded
by lightning he turned away his gaze. But she is

already at his side, has seized his hand with a soft pressure that he cannot withstand, leads him with gentle force, that he must follow, up the bridge, over the wall, down into the inner yard, where his comrades, jubilant, press around him, and at the same time, with a sudden impulse, seize him, raise him up on high, and with jubilation and noise carry the fugitive—the returned one—into the house, as though they would with bantering cunning drive from their prey the demons lurking about the door-sill.

So it also seemed to him. Conrad is back, the best rifle in the colony. They had resolved without Conrad to do their duty. But the quick looks, the short words which they interchanged, the faces illuminated with joy, these said plainly, "It is far better so." If only Aunt Ursul and Christian Ditmar were here the dance might begin at once. "They could be here already," thought Catherine. "Hurrah! there they come!" cried Richard Herkimer, who had gone up on the gallery to see better; "and there are three. The third is the minister. Hurrah! and again, hurrah! and once more, *hurrah!*"

Who now has time or inclination to ask the breathless ones how the minister came to be here? Enough that they are here at the right time, and that at last the bridge can be thrown off and that the door can be barricaded with the strong beams lying ready. There they now are, locked in their wooden fortress in the midst of the wilderness, miles away from friends, depending solely on themselves, on their firm courage, on their strong arms, on their keen eyes—two women, nine men, nine rifles. Though the minister is not to be counted, as he would not know how to use a rifle even if he wished to fight, yet Aunt Ursul has a rifle, and knows how to use it, and will fight; that can be depended on.

Now the parts are assigned and everything and every man is in place. In one division of the lower, thoroughly protected room is Hans, whom Lambert will not sacrifice. In another are the sheep, which were taken in out of compassion, and now bleated piteously in the darkness. On the gallery of the upper story, behind the breastwork, lay Lambert, Richard, Fritz Volz, Jacob Ehrlich and Anton Bierman, with the barrels of their rifles in the port-holes. On the floor above, at the trap-doors of the high, shingled roof, stood Conrad, Aunt Ursul and Christian Ditmar, whose far-carrying rifle was, in his time, the dread of the enemy. With them is the minister, who, though he is not a good shot, well understands how quickly and properly, to load a rifle. This service Adam Bellinger performs for those on the gallery. Catherine is to bring food and drink, when necessary, to those who are to fight. Lambert and the rest have adjured her not in any way to expose herself to danger. She, however, secretly purposed, in case of need, to take Adam's rifle, which now lay idle, and follow Aunt Ursul's example.

Silence reigned in the house. Whoever should see it standing there, still, gloomy, locked, would suppose it forsaken by its former occupants—a piece of abandoned property in the all-embracing wilderness. Silent in its entire circuit lay that wilderness under the ban of the hot afternoon sun. Silent was the green prairie on which scarcely a single flower bent, or grass-stem waved. Silent the woods whose tree-tops reached up unmoved toward the blue sky, from which several white clouds looked down motionless. Deepest silence! Forest stillness!

There!—a loud, long drawn-out, many-voiced whoop, whose dreadful echo is reflected back from surrounding objects. From the forest break forth at once fifty half-naked Indians in their colored war-paint, swinging their rifles and tomahawks, and, leaping forward with wild jumps, hastening over the prairie, one part coming directly toward the block-house, the other going around so as in a short time to rush up from all sides. The house stood as silent as before. There was no reply to the demand which the on-rushing enemy kept repeating with yells and cries and whoops. The first are already within a hundred paces—then comes the answer, a short, sharp sound from four German rifles fired at the same moment, so that but one report was heard. Four Indians fall not to rise again. The others run on more rapidly, and had already reached the surrounding wall, when again is heard the crack of four rifles and again four

Indians fall—one, having been shot through the heart, leapt up high, like a deer.

This they had not expected. A third salvo might follow the second, and there yet lay between them and the house a ditch and wall. Who could tell whether this third salvo might not be more dreadful than the first two? No one wants it tried. In a moment all turn and run, in like haste, back to the woods, which they had not reached until again four shots are sent after them. Two more sink dead at the feet of the French, who had kept concealed in the woods, observing the bloody spectacle before them, full of horror and compelled to confess that the first attack, which they had cunningly left to their Indian allies, had altogether failed.

Yes, the first attack had been repelled. Those in the block-house shook hands with each other, and then again grasped their freshly loaded guns. One of the Indians raised up on his hands and knees, and again fell back, and then again raised up. Richard Herkimer said: "That is my man. The poor devil shall not be in pain much longer." He raised his rifle to his cheek, but Lambert laid his hand on his shoulder saying: "We shall need every shot, Richard, and he has enough." The Indian, in a death-cramp grasped the grass, twitched a few times, and then lay rigid like the rest of his comrades.

"What will happen now? Will they seek us again in the same way, or choose some other mode of attack? and what then?" The young men debated the matter, and Aunt Ursul, who had come down from the upper floor, joined in the discussion. Their views were divided. Lambert thought that they had soon enough found out how strong the fastness was, and how much they must sacrifice in this most dangerous pitfall until the rest should actually reach the house. It also appeared how large the number was, since thus far it was clear that they had had to do with only a part, and that their principal force was still in the woods.

"Lambert is right," said Aunt Ursul. "They are one hundred and fifty strong—fifty French and a hundred Onondagas."

"Ninety-two," said Anton Bierman, "for eight lie there."

Jacob Ehrlich usually laughed when Anton said something witty. This time he did not laugh. He was silently reckoning how many Indians, leaving out the French, would fall to his share if there really were so many. Jacob Ehrlich could not make out the exact number, but he reached the result that under all the circumstances it would be hard work.

The others looked inquiringly at Aunt Ursul. That the report came from Conrad was certain, but how had he learned the fact? Aunt Ursul now related her yesterday's expedition with the minister. But thus it could not be concealed that, without her interference, Conrad would not now have been here.

But about this she did not wish to speak, at least to-day. She also said that Conrad had found and watched the camp of our enemies; that he had counted them head by head, and that they had divided into two parts; that of these the larger, a hundred French, as many Onandagas and at least two hundred Oneidas, had started for the Mohawk, and would doubtless already have arrived, but that the Oneidas had no heart for the affair, and that it was at least possible that at the decisive moment they would fall away and go over to their old treaty friends.

'"If it is so, we can also reckon on help from my father," said Richard Herkimer.

"We will reckon on nobody but ourselves," said Lambert.

"What are the fellows up to now?" said Anton Bierman.

Out of the woods in which the enemy for the last half-hour was entirely concealed there came three men—one Frenchman and two Indians. They had laid aside their arms. Instead of them they carried long rods to the ends of which white cloths were tied. They swung the rods back and forth and made the cloths flutter. So they came up slowly as though they were not quite sure, and wished to assure themselves whether those on the other side were disposed to regard a flag of truce. Anton Bierman and Jacob Ehrlich felt no inclination to do this. They thought that the scoundrels, the year before, had never shown

mercy, and that for their part they would send them
to the devil with their white rags and, though there
were but three, they were worth three charges of
powder. Lambert had enough to do to hush the
excited men, and to make it clear to them that they,
as Germans, should not be the first to do that.

Meanwhile those who had come to ask a parley
had approached to within a short distance of the
house. Lambert appeared on the gallery, after he had
told the others not to let themselves be seen, and
called out: "Halt!"

The three stood still.

"What do you want?"

"Is there one among you who speaks French?"
asked the Frenchman in German.

"We speak only German," answered Lambert.
"What do you want?"

. The Frenchman, a tall, dark-complexioned man,
placed himself in a quite theatrical posture while he
set his flag of truce on the ground with his left hand
and raised the right hand toward heaven, and called
out: ·

"I, Roger de St. Croix, Lieutenant in the service
of his most Christian Majesty, Louis XV., and com-
mander of his majesty's troops here present, and of
the allied Indians of the tribe of the Onondagas,
herewith bring to your knowledge and inform you
that, if you at once and on the spot lay down your
arms and give yourselves up to our mercy or severity,

we will grant life to you, your wives and children, nor will we injure you in your possessions, but will leave everything—house, barn and cattle—undestroyed. But should you be mad enough to make further resistance against the formidable power of six hundred well-armed and disciplined soldiers of his majesty, and as many more brave and dreadful Indians, then I swear—I, Roger de St. Croix—that not one of you shall get away with his life—neither you, nor your wives, nor your children—and that we will level with the dust your houses and barns, so that nobody could again find the place where they stood."

The man, who spoke German glibly enough, though with a French accent, had spoken louder and louder until at last he shrieked. He now let his gesticulating right arm fall to his side and stood there in an indifferent attitude, like a man conducting a spiritless conversation which he can stop or continue just as the other may prefer.

"Shall I answer for you?" asked Anton as he struck his rifle.

"Still!" said Lambert, and then raised his voice: "Go back to your people and tell them that we here, united German men, one as all and all as one, are resolved to hold the house, come what will; and that we are quite confident that we can hold it, even if you were twelve hundred instead of one hundred and fifty, counting in the ten already lying there."

The Frenchman made a quick motion of surprise,

and turned to his attendants who had been standing there without altering their posture, or stirring. He appeared to say something to them which arrested their attention. Then he again took his former theatrical posture and called out:

"From what you last said, though it is false, I infer that there is with you a certain Conrad Sternberg. I promise you that not a hair shall be bent and a hundred Louis d'or besides, if you will deliver to us this Conrad Sternberg."

"The man of whom you speak," replied Lambert, "is with us, and you have already twice heard the crack of his rifle, and if you so please you can hear it again."

"But this Conrad is a traitor, who has cheated us in the most shameful manner," cried the Frenchman.

"I am no traitor," called Conrad, who now stood beside his brother. "I told you I would escape as soon as possible. Since you this time thought your six could hold me you will the next time set a dozen to guard me."

"The next time I will begin by having laid at my feet, first your scalp and then your head," cried the Frenchman in loudest tones.

"Enough!" called Lambert. "I give you ten minutes to get back into the woods. He of you who then yet lets himself be seen outside does it at his peril!"

The Frenchman doubled up his fist, and then bethought himself as to what, under all circumstances, a Frenchman owes himself against German blockheads, and taking off his large, three-cornered hat, made a low bow, turned on his heel, and walked at first slowly, then faster and faster toward the woods, until he fell into a regular trot, evidently to spare the Germans the shame of shooting, after the ten minutes had elapsed, at the messenger of his Most Christian Majesty.

"Lord of my life!" cried Anton. "Now I first know him. That is the same fellow, Jacob, who three years ago came to us begging, and who afterward hung about the neighborhood half a year. He called himself Mr. Emil, and said that he had shot a comrade in a duel and had on that account to flee. But others claimed that he was an escaped galley-slave. Afterward he wanted to marry Sally, Joseph Kleeman's black girl, but she said she was too good for a fellow like that, and Hans Kessel, Sally's treasure, once pounded him as limber as a rag, after which he disappeared. Lord of my life! He gives himself out here as a lieutenant, and speaks of his Most Christian Majesty, and is willing to leave us our dear lives—the mean plate-licker, the gallows-bird!"

So honest Anton scolded and abused, and asserted that if he did not get this Mr. Emil, or Saint Croix, or whatever the fellow's name was, in front of his rifle, to him the whole sport would be spoiled.

The rest would gladly have known what Conrad had

before had to do with the French, but their curiosity
remained unsatisfied, for Conrad had immediately
again gone up, and soon the attention of the besieged
was directed to another side. From the barn-yard
arose a column of smoke, which every moment became thicker and blacker, until the flames burst
forth from the mass. The enemy had made his threat
true. It seemed to be a useless barbarity, for the
barn was too far from the block-house for the flames
to leap across, though the wind, which now began to
rise, was blowing toward the house, driving along
smoke and sparks. But this whole war was only a
continuous chain of such barbarities. This morning
Lambert had mentally seen what he now actually
saw. He had wrought all this with his own hands,
which now the more firmly grasped the barrel of his
gun. Then there cracked a shot above and another,
and Aunt Ursul called down the stairs: "Be watchful!
Eyes left! In the reeds!"

The meaning of these words and of the shots fired
from above soon became clear. The attention of the
besieged had not been uselessly directed to the land
side. In the thick sedge and reeds, of man's height,
with which the shores of the creek were overgrown,
one could come from the woods within a hundred
paces of the house. It was a difficult undertaking,
for the ground was a bottomless bog as far as the
reeds grew, and where they ended the creek was deep
and rapid. But they had ventured to do it, and it

soon appeared with what result.   From among the
reeds here and there shots were soon being fired with
increasing rapidity.   There must indeed have been
a considerable number who had came by that dangerous way, and had concealed themselves along the
shore in spite of all that those in the house could do
to free themselves from neighbors so unwelcome and
dangerous.

Wherever an eagle-feathered head or a naked arm
showed itself, or the barrel of a gun glistened, yes, if
the sedge only moved, a bullet struck.   But though
a few dead bodies floated down the creek, others lay
dead or wounded among the rushes and others still
had sunk in the morass, the remaining number was
so great and the daring enemy was so embittered by
his heavy losses, it seemed that the worst must and
would come.   Besides, the evening wind kept increasing, causing the tops of the rushes to wave hither and
thither, so that it was difficult and often impossible
to follow the movements of the unseen enemy, and
many a precious charge was wasted.   This evidently
made the attacking party more bold.   The fire-line
was constantly receding from the shore.   The more
frequent bullets rained against the breastwork and
roof.   It might be expected at any moment that a
rush would be made from the reeds and that, having
rapidly run across the short distance that still separated them from the house, they would attempt to
storm it.

But it soon became manifest that on the opposite side of the house they were by no means willing to set the decision of the day on a single card. Suddenly, at the edge of the woods, there began to be a stirring and a moving as if the forest itself had become alive. Broad shields of man's height cunningly contrived out of pine branches were pushed out or carried, one could not tell which, in a connected line over the smooth level meadow toward the house. The progress was slow, but onward, until they had approached within rifle shot, and then the marksmen behind the shields opened a lively fire. The shields were indeed no sure protection for the attacking party, but they made the aim of the beleaguered more difficult, and moreover compelled them to be more watchful, and 'to direct their rifles toward two sides at once.

But the oncoming foe had not yet exhausted his ingenuity. From the barn-yard, where everything was entirely burned down, they at the same time came rolling before them Lambert's large casks, and, as soon as they were near enough, they set them up and so made a wall that could every moment be shoved farther, and offered a much more sure protection than the pine-branch shields. Anton Bierman had laughed loudly when he saw the casks coming toward the house, but after he had fired at them a few times, clearly without effect, he laughed no more, but said softly to his friend Jacob: "Things begin to look serious!"

It was indeed serious. So far no one had received

apparent injury, except that one and another was badly cut by splinters torn from the breastwork by bullets, and bled profusely. But the battle had now lasted for three hours. It was a warm piece of work, under the June sun, and the cheeks of the fighters glowed, and the barrels of their guns were hot. Furthermore, many an eye, when it could turn away a moment from the unaccustomed bloody work toward the sun, had observed with care how rapidly it had been sinking during this hour which would not end—how low it already stood. So long as its light lasted a handful of men might keep up the doubtful strife against a crafty, cunning enemy far outnumbering them, and leave it undecided. But how soon the sun would set, and when it did, and darkness came on, it would cover the valley for hours with an impenetrable veil, since now the moon did not rise till after midnight; and under the protection of the night and of the fog the enemy could slip up and storm the place. True the beams of the lower story were thick enough, and the only door was barred, but a dozen axes could in a short time break in the door and, however thick the beams, they could not withstand fire. Then the beleaguered would have no choice but to give their living bodies to the flames, or with their arms in their hands try to open a way from the closely surrounded, burning house. And even then their destruction was sure. Whoever was not killed at once would, on account of the number of the pursuers, be overtaken and brought down.

Such was the situation.   It could not be doubtful
either to the besieged, or besiegers, who had long
been convinced that the house was defended by no
more than ten rifles. But however much this certainty may have raised their desire to fight and their
thirst for vengeance, the courage of those in the block-
house remained unbroken.   Nobody thought of flight,
which was indeed impracticable; nor of surrender,
which equally meant a painful death.   All were resolved to defend themselves to the last breath, and
sooner to kill themselves, or each other, than to fall
alive into the hands of the cruel enemy.

Lambert and Catherine had already before said
this to each other, and during the battle they had
more than once signaled the death covenant to each
other with silent, intelligent glances.   But the courageous girl was—not only to her lover—like a banner
which waves before the bold soldier in battle and on
which his eyes rest with an enthusiasm that over-
comes death   Whoever looked at the pale, still, determined, restlessly helpful maiden, drank from a
spring of courage and strength, so that his fearful
heart beat higher and his tired limbs were again
strengthened.   To the commands constantly repeated
from the first: "Stay away, Catherine! Don't stand
there, Catherine!" she paid no attention.   Where
she knew she was needed, there she was; above with
the men under the hot roof; below with those on the
gallery, giving one a drink; taking a discharged rifle

from the hands of another; giving to another a gun that she herself had loaded. She had also learned quickly, as she learned everything on seeing it, that Adam Bellinger, though he reasonably exerted himself and the sweat ran in streams from his forehead, was not equal to his task, and that the marksmen often called in vain for their guns.

So she was again occupied in the inner room when Aunt Ursul, Conrad, old Christian and the minister came down from above, while also those in the gallery stopped shooting and it became still outside.

"What is going on?" asked Catherine.

"They are about to visit us with a second storming party," said Lambert, coming in from the gallery. "It is well that you have come down. Every man of us must now be on the gallery. We shall soon enough have them under us."

Others also came in to hear what would happen. They were assembled in full count.

"I think," said Lambert, "we had better not shoot until they are on the wall, for now they will not turn back again, and then we have eight of them sure. Afterward five of us will give attention to the others, while the rest put a stop to the work of the scoundrels below us. Are the rifles all loaded?"

"Here!" and, "Here!" said Catherine and Adam, handing out the last two rifles.

It so happened that the two were Lambert's and Conrad's rifles. As they both at the same time came

up it was not by mere chance that both took their
guns with the left hand, for at the next moment their
right hands clasped, and thus they stood before Catherine, who, blushing deeply, took a step back, fearing
that her nearness should anew break the bond of the
brothers. But the minister laid his hand on the
hands of the brothers as they held each other with a
firm grasp, and said: "As these two who had for a
moment lost each other, and in the hour of danger
have again found each other, to be and to remain, in
life and in death and in eternity united, so let us all,
dear brothers and sisters, thank and praise God that
we here stand together so united, and that, in this
solemn hour, which according to all human calculation is our last, we are fulfilling the chief commandment, and are loving one another. Since life can
offer us nothing greater than this, though we should
live a thousand years, let us without murmuring take
our departure from this dear life. We do not give it
up lightly. We have defended it as well as we could.
But we are only flesh and blood, and this our fortress is wood. God, however, who made us in his
own likeness and breathed his breath into us—God is
a spirit and a strong tower."

As the minister uttered the word, then, as though
the Spirit to whom they were praying had inspired it,
the sentiment it awakened passed through the little
assembly and Luther's battle-hymn sounded forth as
if from one mouth:

A strong tower is our God—
A good defense and armor;
He keeps us free in every need
Which us has yet befallen;
The old and angry fiend,
Earnestly he means,
Great might and much craft
His dreadful armor is,
On earth there's nothing like him.

With our own might nothing's done;
We surely are quite helpless;
There fights for us the very Man,   ˏ
Whom God himself has chosen.
Ask you who is He?
He's called Jesus Christ,
The Lord Sabaoth,
There is no other God;
The field he'll not surrender.

And were the world of devils full,
Would they us wholly swallow,
So fear we not so very much;
We yet shall surely prosper.

There they were, on every side, as though the
creek and the prairie and the woods had spit them
out at once.   They came on in wild leaps, swinging
axes and guns and brush-bundles.   French and Indians, hunters and dogs, rushed on to battle.   In a
moment they flew across the narrow intervening
space, down into the ditch, up the wall, in frenzied
motion, digging with their nails, one on another's
shoulder, up, up.

Up but not over—at least not the first.

As soon as a head emerged from behind the wall, a
pair of elbows put firmly on it, a breast exposed,

came the deadly bullet, and the venturesome enemy
fell back into the ditch. This fate befalls the first,
the second, the third and the fourth. The fifth at
last succeeds and the sixth; and now half-a-dozen at
once, and at another point also a couple. These are
enough. The object is gained. Words of command
are called out. Those who are still on the other side
of the wall retire, forming about the house in a double circle and continually firing. Again, and then for
the last time, to rush forward so soon as those who
had pressed to the house should have finished their
work.

It will to all appearance soon be finished. Sharp
axes cut down the door. The ax-swingers understand their work. They have before opened breaches
in many a barricaded house. And those on the other
side, toward which the wind was blowing, understood
their business equally well. They have often before
placed a firebrand against a house they could not
otherwise take. Those above shot well through the
round holes in the bottom of the gallery, and one or
two of those below must pay for their bravery with
their lives. But the others are covered, and the rain
of bullets which pours upon the house divides the
force of the besieged who must turn to every side at
once. Yet a few strokes and the door lies in fragments and out of the thick smoke which comes up
over there the flame will soon burst forth.

The beleaguered know it. An attempt to avert the

threatened danger must be made.   They must risk a
sally.   Two of them must do it.   Which two?

"I!" called out the brave minister.   "Why is it
not suitable for me?"

I!" cried Conrad.   "This is my business!"

Conrad's and mine," said Lambert with determined voice, "and no one else.   Away, the rest of
you, to your posts.   You, Richard and Fritz, guard the
door.   Here are the two axes; and now, in God's
name—"

The beams which bar the door are taken away so
as to uncover a strong plank, fitting closely into the
opening and against which the blows from without
are directed, the door having been shattered.   The
last beam is drawn away; the plank falls; the breach
desired by the besiegers is made, and out of the
breach rush Lambert and Conrad side by side, old
Christian Ditmar swinging aloft an ax with his nerv-
ous arm and crying: "Here!   Germany forever!"

It is the first word that has to-day fallen from his
lips, and it is his last for to-day and forever.   Pierced
at once with three bullets, cut and crushed by a dozen
knife cuts and ax-blows he falls, but his big-hearted
purpose is attained.   He broke the first onset of the
attacking party.   He made a way for the two young
men behind him.   They rushed into this passage-way.
Nothing can withstand Conrad's giant strength.   His
blows fall like hail.   He rages among the crowd like
a jaguar among sheep.   Yes, it is a jaguar that has

come among them—the great jaguar, as they call him at the lake, who had already torn so many of the tribe of Onondagas. They are willing to fight with the devil himself, but cannot bear to look at the flaming eyes of the great jaguar. They rush away toward the wall, over the wall, into the ditch, followed by Conrad. Lambert, who had already pulled apart the burning pile of wood, called after him that he should go no farther but come back, for the others, who had seen the shameful flight of their comrades, now directed their fire at the two. Bullet after bullet strikes the wall near Lambert. It is a wonder that he is yet uninjured; yes, that he is alive. But he does not think of himself. He only thinks of his lion-hearted brother. He rushes toward the raging one, who is fighting near the wall with three Indians, the last within the enclosure. They shall not get over it again. He seizes one, whirls him on high and dashes him against the wall where the unlucky fellow lies with a broken neck. The two others improve the moment and climb over the wall. One of them, before sliding down into the ditch, discharges his gun.

"Come in, for God's sake, Conrad!" called Lambert. He seizes Conrad by the hand and drags him away. They had reached the door when Conrad staggered like a drunken man. Lambert caught him about the body.

"It is nothing, dear brother," said Conrad and straightened himself up. But in the door he fell down. A stream of blood gushed from his mouth and moistened the door-sill which he had sworn never again to cross without the shedding of his blood.

The door is again barred more strongly than before.

The fire that Lambert had pulled apart wastes away powerless at the base of the house. The house is saved; but how long? The little company that guards it is poorer by two fighting men. The rest, exhausted by their frightful labor, are more dead than alive. The ammunition is used up to within a few charges, and the sun pours its last red rays over the lonely battle-field in the midst of the surrounding forest. In a few minutes it will go down. Night—the last night—will come on.

"Your brother is dead," said the minister to Lambert.

"He has gone before us," said Lambert. "Stay near me, Catherine."

The minister and Catherine had been occupied below with Conrad. The minister was skilled in the healing art, but here his skill could accomplish nothing. Conrad had opened his beautiful blue eyes, with a bewildered look, but once. They for a moment became bright and clear, as he saw Catherine's face through the mist of death. Then he lay still with closed eyes. There was deep peace in the yet wild and battle-angered face. He breathed but once again. Then his head sunk to one side as if he were now sleeping quietly. The sun sinks behind the forest, spreading its blood-red evening-light over those on the gallery.

"On what do the fellows wait?" asked Jacob Ehrlich.

"Eternity will be long enough for you, fool," replied Anton Bierman.

"If father means to send us succor he must be quick about it," said Richard Herkimer, with a sad smile.

"Hurrah! hurrah! and again hurrah!" cried Adam Bellinger, who now rushes down the stairway and dances about like a crazy person, and then, crying loudly, falls into the minister's arms.

"Poor boy! poor boy!" said the minister.

Lambert went round to the other side of the gallery, from which one could look down the creek to the edge of the woods where the road makes a turn and then disappears to reappear for a short distance a little further on. On this side and on that there was nothing in the road. The slight hope which had kindled in Lambert's breast was at once extinguished. Sadly he shook his head.

And yet, what sound is that? Lambert clearly hears a dull, strong sound, while, at the same moment, the noise of the enemy is stilled. The sounds become heavier and stronger. Lambert's heart beats as though it would split.

Suddenly there came around the corner of the woods one, two, three riders in full run and a moment later a large company; twenty, thirty horses, under whose hoofs the ground trembles. The riders swing their rifles and "Hurrah! hurrah!" sound forth so that Lambert hears.

He hastens to his comrades. "Have you all loaded? Then up and out! Now it is our turn. Now we will drive them!"

A sharp pursuit—a wild pursuit on the darkening prairie after the French and Indians, who in frenzied flight rush toward the woods while German rifles crack after them.

CHAPTER XVI

It was during the fifth summer after these events that the August sun, which rose above the woods in beaming glory, brought the Germans on the creek, on the Mohawk and on the Schoharie, a joyful day. To-day bison and deer might go their way through the primitive forest unmolested. The hunter drew the charge out of his rifle and put into it a large load of loose powder. To-day cattle and sheep were left to themselves in the pasture-fields. The herdsman had brushed his Sunday-coat clean, and had stuck a large bunch of flowers in his hat. To-day there was rest from pressing labor, in field and mart. The farmer, much as he had to do, the herder, the hunter, and all the world, young and old, men, women and children, were to keep a great holiday—a great, wondrous, fine peace-festival. For there was again peace on earth—which had drunk the blood of her children in streams for seven long years. Peace over in the old home; peace here in the new one. There the hero of the century, old Fritz, the great Prussian king, was done with his enemies, and had sheathed his sword. So here too the battle-ax could be buried.

During the last years it had indeed become dull enough. Since, in the spring of 'fifty-eight, the attack of the French and Indians had been so bravely resisted by the Germans, they had made no further invasion across the border, protected as it was by such a warlike race. As now Fort Frontenac had fallen and Quebec was surrendered the following year. England's great victory was won, and what yet followed were only the flying sparks and the last flickering of a great conflagration. But for a German shingle or straw roof sparks are also dangerous, and the master of the house had yet constantly gone to bed burdened with anxiety, and the next morning went to his labor with his rifle on his shoulder Now the last trace of uncertainty had disappeared, and the bell in the little church sounded out "Peace, peace," over sunny fields and still woods.

Out of the woods and over the fields they came in festive groups, on foot, on horseback, young and old, adorned with flowers, sending friendly greetings from afar, heartily shaking each other's hands if they happened to meet at the cross roads; engaging in friendly conversation as they went through the smiling valley between the Mohawk and the creek toward the hill on which the church stood, which to-day could not hold all who came with pious thankfulness.

"But God does not dwell in temples made by human hands. He is clothed with light. Heaven is His throne and the earth is His footstool." That is the text of the sermon which the worthy minister, Rosenkrantz, to-day delivers to his congregation, gathered

around him in a wide circle under the bright sky and
on the green earth.   In words that fly on eagle's wings
over the assembly he praises the great, good God, on
whom they, in their need, had called, and who, out
in the wild woods and on the lonely prairie, had delivered them from danger.   He calls to remembrance
those who had fallen during the war, and says that
not in vain did they shed their precious blood for
house and home in which man must live, that in the
circle of his own family, at his own hearth, he may
show the virtues of love, of helpfulness and patience,
and live according to the image of Him who made
him.   He declares that those who survive are called
and chosen, after the fearful labor of the war, to the
valuable works of peace, and that all hatred and quarreling and envy and strife must henceforth be ban-
ished from the congregation, otherwise the dead would
rise and complain and ask: "Why did we die?"

More than once the voice of the minister trembled
with deep feeling.   He had gone through it all himself.   Every word came from the bottom of his heart
and so it reached the heart.   There was scarcely one
of the assembled hundreds whose eyes remained free
from tears;   and when the benediction was pro-
nounced, that the Lord who had now so evidently
let the light of His countenance fall on them and had
given them peace, might also further bless and preserve them and give them peace, Amen! the word
touched every heart,   and hundreds of voices re-

sponded: "Amen!" "Amen!" as the wind roars through the tops of the trees of the forest. Then the roaring grew louder and mightier, as it spread in sacred accord over the sunny fields in the hymn. "Now let us all thank God."

Then they retired stiller than they came.

But the festival of peace should also be one of joy, and there were with the old far too many who were young to keep in their joy very long. At first a few lively words were jokingly interchanged. Then a lusty fellow had a funny conceit which, in that beautiful, bright sunshine, he could not possibly keep to himself. The old smiled. The young men laughed. The girls giggled. The laughter and the joyfulness were so inspiring and communicative that the guns went off as if of themselves, and an hour later one who did not know better might have thought that Herkimer's house, which the French had not ventured to attack in the frightful years of '57 and '58, was being stormed on the festival of peace by German young men.

This indeed was unnecessary. Nicolas Herkimer's large and hospitable house had to-day all its doors opened wider than usual, for men and women—for all who lived on the Mohawk, on the creek and on the Schoharie—for all that were German, or that were ready to rejoice with the Germans—all were invited, and were welcome to drink of Nicolas Herkimer's beer and eat of his roast, and, happy with the joyful, help to celebrate the great festival. As all had been invited so nobody stayed at home, unless it might be a mother who could not leave her children alone, or one to whom it was utterly impossible to come. Big John Mertens had come, and, simpering, mingled with the guests, his thumbs in the pockets of his long vest, except when he drew somebody aside secretly to ask him if it was not very nice in John Mertens that he gave precedence to Nicolas Herkimer, and that he did honor to his festival by his presence; that he could just as well entertain such a multitude of guests and perhaps a little better. Hans Haberkorn was there, and acted very modestly and reminded one and another that he had then already said that three ferries across the river were not too many. Now there were six ferrymen and all made a good living. Some thought that Hans Haberkorn talked in that way because he was owing Nicolas Herkimer every cent that the ferry and beer-house were worth, and a couple of hundred dollars besides. But who had time now to investigate such things?

Surely not the young men and maidens who, on the level ground adjoining the house, beneath the shadow of an immense basswood tree, were ceaselessly swinging in the dance to the stirring music of a violin, two fifes and a drum. Parents and old people, who sat under the long, projecting roof where it was cool, and thoughtfully emptied one pitcher after another, had also something better for their entertainment. They remembered, as to-day they well might, what they themselves had suffered in the home across the sea, or had, at least, been told by the father, or the grandfather—how the bitter enemy, the Frenchman, had scorched and burned, up and down the beautiful green Rhine, and how their own lord by his servants had seized what the French had left, so that, in his grand castles, he with his courtiers might gormandize and have brilliant feasts and great hunts, while the poor farmers, oppressed by service and burdens of every kind, were starving of sheer hunger. And also the priesthood and the tithes and other endless miseries of the holy Roman empire of the German nation. Yes, yes, it had looked badly over there, and though since the great king of Prussia, old Fritz, had intervened and had followed bravely on his crutch, it was a great deal better, yet one could live here freer and better, if one considered it well, being under no lord; and the minister, though all were not like Rozenkrantz, would allow one to talk with him and a man's life could be joyful, especially now that the Frenchman has crept into his hole and the war is at an end.

Then they talked about the war. That was an inexhaustible subject. In that everybody had taken part—had himself fought and had his part to tell—his altogether peculiar experiences, which, if to no one else, at least to the narrator were of deep interest. They recalled the chief events of the war.

wherein all agreed that the interest was supreme. These were recounted a hundred times and were gladly repeated once more, and which clothed themselves in a wonderful garb, though the eye-witnesses were yet for the most part alive.

Of these peculiarly noteworthy events, none was more remarkable than the battle at Sternberg's house in the year '58. And when the deed had been told that nine men had for six or seven hours resisted one hundred and fifty well-armed enemies, incredible as it was, there was that in the history which gave it for the moment a romantic color, even in the eyes of the indifferent. The quarrel of the brothers over the beautiful maiden, who was now the handsomest wife in the whole district; the reconciliation of the brothers in the last hour, and the succeeding heroic deaths of Christian Ditmar and of Conrad Sternberg—the oldest and the youngest of the company—and both dying so nobly that one could not do better than to follow them, as Aunt Ursul said, when they were both laid in the cool earth. Yes, she had soon enough followed them—the wonderfully brave souls —she who was so rough, while her heart was so soft that she did not want to live longer, nor could she without her husband, with whom she had spent forty years in joy and sorrow—but mostly in scrrow—and without her wild, strong and last but perhaps most dearly beloved son. Yes, yes, that he was, to Aunt Ursul—the Indian, and, as they already before had

called him and still called him at the lake, the great
jaguar—Conrad Sternberg, wild and strong. Were
he still living Cornelius Vrooman, from Schoharie,
would not have carried off the victory away from the
young men on the Mohawk. What Cornelius did
was indeed no small matter, to draw a sleigh by the
tongue, standing in the sand, loaded with twelve
heavy men, half a foot from its position. Conrad
would have drawn the sleigh five feet with Cornelius
on his shoulders. Yes, yes, Conrad Sternberg was
endowed with superhuman strength. Would he otherwise have been able to overcome twenty-four Indians
who had already pressed forward to the house? And
was it not more than human courage for him, whom
every Onondaga had sworn to kill, notwithstanding
to go to their camp and set the Onondagas and Oneidas against each other and both against the French
and then to deliver himself up to the Onondagas, as
they insisted on it that they might feel assured, and
to tell them that he would stay with them as long as
they could hold him; and the simpletons, who might
have known better, had thought that six men were
sufficient for this, and had placed the six, with Conrad
as guide, in the van. Yes, he had showed them the
way there whence none of them would return. So
had he protected the Sternberg house, and, if one
correctly considered it, all the houses on the creek
and the Mohawk, since the Oneidas went back, and
the French and Onondagas might be glad that they

had not in the evening been followed more sharply, since half of the cavalry had been sent to relieve the Sternberg house. Yes, that was a man, that Conrad, the like of whom would probably never again appear among them—a Samson among the Philistines, "who slew them with the jaw-bone of an ass," as the minister to-day said, in his sermon, though he did not mention Conrad's name. The minister himself knew how to tell about it, for he was there and could say more if he would; but he said no more about it, as soon as he came in his discourse to the chapter. Now, perhaps a servant of peace should not be blamed if he did not wish to remember that he had laid low six Indians that day with his own hand. In their gossiping exaggeration and envy they proceeded to add that if Lambert Sternberg seldom speaks of his brother he may possibly have his grounds, since many suspect that Catherine loved Conrad better than him, and that Lambert Sternberg, in spite of his comfortable condition—since he is now also Aunt Ursul's heir —and in spite of his handsome wife and beautiful children, is the unhappiest man in the whole valley.

"Be still! There comes Lambert with Herkimer; and what peculiar little fellow have they forked up?"

Nicolas Herkimer and Lambert Sternberg approached these confident dividers of honors, whose conversation had just taken so interesting a turn, and introduced to them Mr. Brown, of New York, who in Albany, where he had business, had heard of the

peace-festival on the Mohawk, and as he was a friend
of the Germans, had at once decided to come up and
help them celebrate the day.

The honor-conveyers welcomed the stranger, and
said that it was a great honor which they knew how
to prize, and asked whether Mr. Brown and Lambert
—Herkimer had already gone away—would not sit
down at their table and empty a glass to the well-being of his majesty the king.   Mr. Brown was ready
for this, and also drank to the welfare of the Germans, but then left, with the promise that later he
would come again with Lambert; that he wished first
to look about a little over the place where the festival
was being held.

Mr. Brown had not made the long journey from
New York to Albany and from Albany here merely on
his own business, nor out of pure sympathy with the
Germans.   He came at the suggestion of the Government, which had at last comprehended the value of
the German settlements on the Mohawk, and further
up toward the lake, and had formed the earnest purpose to advance them as far as possible.   Mr. Brown,
being peculiarly fitted to further this end on account
of his long business intercourse with the Germans,
was intrusted with this mission.

He was to communicate with the leading Germans,
such as Nicolas Herkimer and Lambert Sternberg,
and take their proposals into consideration.   To this
end he had held a long conference with Nicolas Her-

kimer, and now imparted his views to his younger
friend while walking with him about the place. Lambert attentively listened in silence. It did not occur
to him that the Englishman had in reality the interests of his nation in his eye when he spoke of the ad-
vantages which should grow out of it all to the Germans. Nor did Mr. Brown deny it.

"We are a practical people, my dear young friend,"
said he, "and do nothing for God's sake. Business
is business; but this is an honorable one—I mean
one by which both sides are the gainers. Naturally
you will at first serve as a dike and a protecting wall
against our enemies, the French. You will help extend and establish our control of the continent which
will yet come to us. But if you so pull the chestnuts
out of the fire for us will not the sweet fruits be just
as good for you? When you strike for King George
do you not just as well fight for your own house and
home? What then, man? So long as one does not
stand firm in his own shoes one must lean against
others. See that you Germans reach a position so
that you can enter the market of the world, dealing
for your own advantage and in view of your own danger. You will have to be satisfied either to be taken
in tow by us, or, if you prefer, be road-makers and
pioneers for us."

The earnest man had, according to his custom, at
last spoken very loud, and with it gesticulated with
his little lean arms, and thrust his Spanish cane into

the ground. Now he looked around frightened, grasped Lambert under the arm, and, while he let himself be led farther away, proceeded in a more gentle manner and in lower tones:

"And now I will intrust you with something, my young friend, which I would not for all the world should come to Mrs. Brown's ears, and which also, on your own account, you may keep to yourselves. You remember, Lambert, how five years ago, you were in New York, and we stood on the quay and saw your country people leave the ship, poor simpletons! It rained powerfully, and the dismal scene did not by this means become brighter. Well, this morning, while we were here wandering about, I have been constantly forced to think and have said to myself: What immeasurable life-vigor must stick in this race, which needs but a single life-time to change from half-starved, shy-looking, all-enduring slaves, into lusty, broad-shouldered, independent freemen. How immeasurably must such a race have suffered to sink so deep! How high it must rise when these sufferings are removed; when its good instincts are left to themselves; when fortune permits it freely to unfold its great strength which slumbers hidden and is yet scarcely waked up! How high it must ascend! How wide it must spread! What is beyond its reach? Do not laugh at me, my young friend. I tremble when I think of it—when I think what a host like this, as yet without leaders, only subject to the law of gravity, can overcome—*must* overcome—when it has learned to take care of itself; to lead and to march in rank and file. However this may be, so much is already clear to me; you who here stand on the border are evidently now our vanguard. You prepare your countrymen a way. You are truly German pioneers. But again, not a word of this when you this fall come to New York. My neighbors already call me 'the Dutchman' and Mrs. Brown will not again—Well, as we are now speaking of the women, where, then, is your wife, with whom you at that time so hastily went away? I think I will to-morrow lay claim to your guest-friendship for a day, and so would be gladly introduced to my beautiful entertainer."

"My wife," said Lambert, "is not here. She—"

"I understand, I understand," interrupted the talkative old man. "Little household events happen in the best of families. I understand."

"Now," said Lambert, laughing, "our youngest is already half-a-year old, and my wife was unwilling longer to stay away from the children; and besides, this joyous day is also one of sorrowful thoughts to my family."

"I know, I know," said the old man. "Your brother—we heard of it in New York. What do you want, man? Your brave deed is in the mouth of the people. The ballad singers sing it on the streets:"

"A story, a story,
Unto you I will tell,
Concerning a brave hero—"

"I should say, two brave heroes. But the people like to keep to one. You must tell me all this circumstantially when I come to your house to-morrow."

"This I will cheerfully do," replied Lambert, "and so I will to-day take my leave of you. The sun is already low, and I would like to be home in good time."

Lambert took the old man to the giver of the feast, who sent his hearty compliments to his wife, and promised to come with the guest to-morrow, to have farther consultation, and to visit his daughter-in-law on the way, who had already fourteen days ago presented him with a grandson. Richard, after Aunt Urusl's death, had bought the property from Lambert, and was now his nearest neighbor. Richard came up and proposed to accompany Lambert. Fritz and August Volz would probably also have done this, but their wives did not yet want to leave the festival, which was now at its highest point. And then the women had taken it into their heads that this was the day on which their brother Adam must lose his long-maintained freedom and lay it down at the feet of Margaret Bierman, Anton Bierman's sister. Adam came up. His eyes were red. He no longer stood quite firm on his long legs. He put his arms around Lambert, and assured him with hot tears that a man has but one heart to give once for all, but that if it was necessary for Lambert's comfort—a necessity that he fully understood—to follow Jacob

Ehrlich's example, given a short time before, he would marry a Bierman even if a man has but one heart, and Margaret didn't sound half as nice as a certain other name, that should not cross his lips, "for a man has but one heart and his heart—"

Here came Anton Bierman and his brother-in-law Jacob to fetch the faithless knight, and Anton, who had overheard the last words, assured Lambert that Adam was a perfect fool, though at bottom a good-hearted and brave fellow, and that the old Bellingers had left behind, besides the visible property, a nice round sum, and that if his sister Gretchen was willing he was satisfied. What did Lambert say to it?

Lambert said, that he had always given Adam that advice and would also do it under present circumstances; and to the same effect he spoke to Richard Herkimer as, two hours later, they two trotted up the creek.

"Adam," said he, "is not so great a fool. The fellow has mother wit enough, and, if he can be easily teased, so his antagonists for the most part do not escape without some scratches. He is also brave, when he must be. That he showed at that trying time in the block-house. In wedlock one must be brave. Therefore I always advise to found a new home when it is suitable. And then, Richard, the German only increases when he has his own hearth, when he can care and work for house and home, for wife and child. So I salute the smoke that rises from a new hearth like a banner about which will gather a group of German pioneers, as Mr. Brown calls them, who lead forward the host that shall come after us."

Richard looked at his companion with some astonishment. Lambert had always so few thoughts and words. He would have liked to ask whether Lambert expected to be one among the coming host, but they had just reached his house, and Lambert bade him give his compliments to Annie, pressed his hand and trotted away.

Yes, Lambert always had but few thoughts for others, but not for Catherine. He could tell her everything that his warm heart suggested and about which his ever active mind was busy. She, the handsome, good, intelligent one understood it, felt as he did, and often made things clear that he could not himself see through. What would she say to the proposition that Mr. Brown had made to him? "On, Hans, old fellow, yet a little trot."

Hans was satisfied. The five years had not weakened his strength. He could, if a long, sharp trot was necessary, yet make a round of ten miles with any horse.

But this time the well-known endurance of the active horse was not put to the test. He had scarcely trotted two hundred yards and was beginning to enjoy it, when his master, with a sudden jerk, held him up, and at the next moment sprang out of the saddle.

"Catherine!"

"Lambert!"

"How are the children?"

"All well. Conrad did not want to go to bed before he had seen you."

"And little Ursul?"

"To-day got her third tooth."

"And little Catherine?"

"Sleeps wonderfully."

They walked on along the bank side by side, leading Hans by the bridle.

"Are you yet thinking about it?" said Catherine.

Lambert did not need to ask about what he should be thinking. One does not forget things like that. It seemed as though it had occurred but yesterday.

And yet there had been great changes since that evening. Where they then walked along the seldom-trodden meadow-path they now went through waving grain fields on a well-beaten road in which a deep, firm wagon-track was cut. There were fields with suitable buildings in all directions, as far as the edge of the woods, which in many places had been cleared far back. Where portions of the old wood pasture showed themselves between the cultivated fields, there large gates had been put, over which here and there a colt or a heifer coming up looked with large, languid eyes, while farther on in the pasture the rest were feeding in the rank grass. On through meadows and fields were seen the shingle roofs of large farmsteads, beside which the old barns which had been burned down would have looked very mean. On the place where the block-house was, there now stood forth a stately stone-house in whose gable the windows were glowing in the evening sun.

Yes, there have been great changes since that evening which to Lambert seemed like yesterday, as though he had never lived without his wife and children.

They had put Conrad to bed, and Catherine with her soft voice had sung the wild boy to sleep, while the other two little ones, with their red cheeks, were slumbering quietly in their beds. They sat before the door in the honeysuckle-arbor, through which the soft, summer evening wind was murmuring.

Lambert told his wife the events of the day, and about Mr. Brown, and they discussed Mr. Brown's plan of extending the German settlements farther up the creek, over to the Black River—if possible to Oneida Lake—and that Mr. Brown, Nicolas Herkimer and himself were to buy the land, and that he was to be the leader and patron of the new settlers. He also told Catherine what the old man had said about the future of the Germans in America, and how the Englishman feared that this hardy, industrious race would yet surpass the English and take from them their dominion over the continent.

"Such language from the mouth of so intelligent a man might make us very proud," said Catherine.

"So I thought too," said Lambert. "And yet, when I reflect upon it more fully it makes me quite sad."

"How do you mean, Lambert?"

"I mean the industry, the pains, the labor, the strength, the courage, the energy, we must use to carry it so far here will be such that they might perhaps better remain in the old home. As you have painted your father to me, mild, generous, helpful, learned; such as was my father, quick, decided, looking far ahead; such as was Uncle Ditmar, unbending, stern and refractory; such as was our noble Conrad and Aunt Ursul. What precious blood this new land has already drunk and in the future will drink! And does it produce the right fruit from the costly seed? I know not. Granted that we attain all which our old friend promises us—though it sounds like a fable—but granted that we reach it, and that we should once have to divide the rich inheritance with the English, should we remain Germans? I doubt it, and you yourself, Catherine, have taught me to be doubtful. What would I be without you? And you had to come to me from the old home—could come only from the old home. In your soul there sounds a deeper, purer tone, just as in the beautiful songs that you brought over with you. Will a still deeper tone sound in the souls of our children? What will be their condition should it die out?"

Lambert was silent. Catherine leaned her head on

his shoulder. She found no answer to a question that had already filled her breast with sad anxiety.

"And so," Lambert continued, "my heart is divided into two parts. To-morrow, when the old friend comes, I will go out with him into the woods and show him the way by which those who are to come must go, and point out the places where they must build their huts. But as for myself, I would rather tear down the huts and take you and the children—how goes the song, Catherine, with which you just now sung our boy to sleep, the dear, old song, out of the dear, old home—

> "Were I a wild falcon,
> I would soar aloft."

And he pointed toward the east where, in the holy mother-arms of the dark night, the glory of the coming day was slumbering.

THE END